The Fear

The Adventures of Silver Dove, Book Nine

Eliza Scalia

Dedicated to Paul Dalton, the love of my life
who helped me get rid of my own fears.

Chapter One
Colomba-
Practice
Session

The practice sword I hold swings down in a swift, graceful arc that is aimed directly at the head of my practice partner Jeff, my martial arts instructor. He misses getting hit right in the skull by placing his own practice weapon in the way only seconds before I hurt him, just like the expert he is. The sound of our two wooden practice weapons creates a harsh cracking sound that seems to echo all around us in the dojo. We are the only two here at the moment, the usual class ended almost an hour ago and Jeff is giving me my own private lessons.

"That was pretty good, you almost got me." He gives me a mischievous smirk that shows that he has an idea up his sleeve. "Now let's see how well you do at defense." He doesn't waste a second, his sword immediately swings forward, and I move myself out of the way. The practice sword swings so close to me that I feel the wind rush by as the sword misses the tip of my nose by only a centimeter. The next strike I am more prepared for. He swings to swipe me across the neck, but I put my sword in between his sword and me before I move forward, twist the sword in my grip so that the pommel, or bottom, of the sword is facing towards Jeff, and I stop myself from hitting Jeff in the face with the pommel by only an inch. He lowers his sword, showing me that he has surrendered. Jeff glances over to the wall where a clock is placed, clearly showing us that our time is up.

"It is about time for your grandmother to come and get you. Let's start cleaning up." I nod at him and the two of us start picking up our other practice weapons in silence for a few moments before Jeff speaks up. "Colomba, I have something to ask that I'm afraid may offend you, but I feel that it needs to be said." I look over at him, immediately curious by his words.

"Yes, what is it?" Jeff looks at me carefully for a second, as if he is trying to figure out how to word what he needs to say.

"You have been acting very... strange these last few months and it seems to be getting worse." I narrow my eyes in confusion as I look at him, worry clouding his gaze.

"What do you mean?" He glances down, apparently embarrassed by what he's about to say.

"Usually, you are very happy and chipper, over the past few months though you seem to have been getting more and more sad, as well as angry. I usually don't see these emotions in you, and it is worrying me." He stares at me, waiting for an answer, but this time I am the one to glance down, embarrassed with myself.

I know why I am upset, but I could never tell him. Earlier this year, I found out a terrible secret having to do with the Dove Pin that I wear that gives me my powers as Silver Dove. I found out that the people who wear the pins are destined to fall in love with each other, meaning I am going to love the Crow one day, my worst enemy. How could Jeff understand the pain I am feeling? How could anybody understand for that matter? How could anybody understand that I am feeling more hopeless than I have ever felt in my life? I feel as if I have no control over my life anymore because of the pin that I used to love, now I feel a little sick whenever I put it on in the morning. I don't want to be connected to it anymore because of what the pin will make happen, but I know that I need to keep using it to protect people from the Crow, the guy who I will love one day. I throw up a little in my mouth at the thought of that.

Apparently, I am letting my feelings get the better of me though since I am letting it show too much and I don't want to worry anybody, especially since none of them can help me, they cannot change my fate. Looking into Jeff's worried face though, I know that if I did tell him, he would try his best to help me.

"I'm okay, I just have a lot on my mind. There's nothing to be worried about, I will figure it out." Jeff nods at me with a sad smile, with that smile I know that I haven't fooled him. He knows that there is much more to it than that, but he can also see that I won't be telling him any time soon, or any time at all. He gives me a simple nod and the two of us continue to put our stuff away while I feel my heart sinking further into my chest as the thought of the Crow circles around in my head, like a hawk circling a mouse it intends to devour. Even though I always try to remain positive, I can't seem to think of anything positive, I feel lost.

Chapter Two
Luis-
A Holiday Is
Coming

Walking down the street as I head to my uncle's antique store, I look at all the decorations hanging up in store windows. Paper cut outs of black cats, witches on broomsticks, and various other monsters seem to be in every storefront. While I look at the decorations, a chilly breeze comes up from behind me, making me shiver and pull my scarf tighter around my face to try and stay warm. Halloween is only a few days away and I can already feel the excitement. I've always loved Halloween. It's a time of year when you can pretend to be someone you're not. As someone who has always been bullied and picked on, pretending to be someone else always seems pretty nice. I always do my best when it comes to my costume, and nobody has ever been able to make fun of my costumes yet since they are always that good. Not even Alex has found an insult for my costumes. The past few years I have dressed as a werewolf, an alien, and a demon.

All of them were pretty frightening, I felt pretty proud that I had made them myself. This year I want to do something different though. Colomba told me what she plans to dress up as, and I want to kind of match her costume. It will take some work, but I'm willing to do that to give her a nice surprise.

I make it to my Uncle Diego's shop, stepping inside I see him sitting at the front counter, polishing a silver tea set. The look of concentration fades from his face when he sees me, replaced with a friendly grin.

"Hello Tigre, where have you been today?" I smile back at him, still feeling the excitement for Halloween pumping in my veins.

"I was out seeing if I could find any more stuff to add to my costume. I'm almost done making it and I want it to be perfect." He raises an eyebrow at me with curiosity.

"You have always put a lot of effort into your costumes Tigre, but you've been doing a lot more this year than with any others. What is so different about this one?" I lower my gaze from his as I try to hide the smile on my face. I haven't told him about my plan for my costume yet, and I don't want to tell him until I have succeeded. I will only say what happens if it goes well for me. Things have never gone well with me with girls and my uncle seems to pity me about that, so I don't want to make him pity me more if it doesn't work out well.

"I don't really have a reason, I just really want to do a good job on it." Uncle Diego nods at me with a skeptical look on his face as he continues to polish the silver tea set while I head upstairs to our apartment. I walk into my room, grab the tv remote, and turn it on so that I can have something to listen to while I get my laundry sorted and get some things done for the preparation of my costume. As I set the stuff for my costume down and start going through my clean clothes in the basket on my bed, I am greeted by the calm, bored sounding voice of a newswoman.

"And in other news, last night the citizens of Drew's Hollow were able to experience another feat of heroism by the mysterious Silver Dove." My chore is instantly forgotten as I turn around to look at the screen. The newswoman is sitting at a desk with a picture of Silver Dove beside her. In the picture, Silver Dove is pulling a kid out of the lake in the town park. The kid is practically crying with joy in the picture while Silver Dove is looking down at him with love, like a protective parent. "Last night a young child ran out of his home to try and swim with his friends in the town's lake only to start drowning. Silver Dove arrived just in time to save the child before his untimely demise. I'm sure that youth will think twice about taking a swim again, and will always be grateful to our hero, Silver Dove. In other news, our local high school football team-" I shut off the tv before the newswoman can continue and throw the remote onto my bed. Even though the tv is now a blank screen, my mind still sees that image of Silver Dove with that loving look in her eyes. The same look she gives all of my soldiers when she is convincing them to stop. It makes me sick.

As that image sticks in my head, my thoughts remind me of something that Shadow told me a few months ago. It was Valentine's Day and I had given the Flying Ace the power to make people fall in love so that I could make Colomba fall in love with me. I decided to stop that though since it didn't feel right to have Colomba like that, it felt like I was living a lie since she only loved me because of a spell. When I got home, I talked to Shadow and she told me something that made my stomach churn with disgust and misery. Shadow told me that the two people who share the medals, The Crow Medal and the one for Silver Dove are destined to fall in love with each other. I couldn't believe it when she said it. How on earth could I fall in love with an annoying girl like her when I am in love with the most amazing girl in the world? Who in their right mind would choose Silver Dove over a girl like Colomba? You would have to be either crazy or stupid to do that, and I am neither crazy nor stupid. I don't get it; I don't get it at all. Why is this happening to me? Why is it that when I am finally close to the girl I care about, I am told that I am supposed to be with somebody else?

Looking back down at the blank screen again, I feel the same anger flood through my veins at the thought of that winged idiot Silver Dove. Shadow was wrong, there is no other explanation. Shadow is wrong and everything will be alright. My plan will succeed, and I will be happy. I will be with Colomba one day no matter what anybody else thinks. I will be with the girl I love. I just need to keep believing that and everything will be fine. I need to keep believing that and try to forget about what Shadow said. As I look at the dark screen of the tv though, I realize that that is going to be a lot harder than it sounds.

Chapter Three
Colomba-
Another Day
Is Here

I squeeze in between a few people in the crowded hallway as I make my way to my next class. All around the halls I can see decorations of white ghosts made of sheets, pumpkins cut out of paper, and a large banner hanging across the hallway saying "Happy Halloween". Halloween is in only two days away and everyone is excited since the school will be having a big dance to celebrate. All day, the only things I've been hearing people talk are what they are dressing up as for the dance, what they want to do at the dance, and who they are going with. The last part seems to be the most important thing since everyone seems to be talking about that more than anything else.

I may be a Junior in high school, but I still get excited for Halloween like a little kid. I already have my costume planned out, and I plan on going to the dance, but I don't have anyone to go with, at least not as a date. I'm okay with just going there with some friends of mine and having a good time. I don't understand why every other girl is so obsessed about it. They act as if it is the most important thing in the world. There is one guy I know though who seems to think the same way. He seems to think that having a girl with him there is more important than anything else. I shouldn't say "girl" though since his attention seems to only be on me.

"Hey Colomba!!" I groan softly as I recognize the voice of Alex. Speak of the devil. Alex rushes through the crowd to get to me, not even apologizing to any of the people that he bumps into to get to me. "How are you doing beautiful? You excited about the Halloween dance? You have a date for it yet?" He moved a little closer to me with a mischievous grin when he asked that last question. He's obviously hoping that I will say no so that he can ask me to go with him for the billionth time over this past week. I want to lie and tell him that I am going with someone, but I know that if I tell him that then he will do anything to figure out who I am going with and then he will probably do something to that guy in revenge. I don't know what he will do, but after learning more about him in the few years I've known him, I can see him doing something bad to whoever he wants revenge against. I pity whoever gets on Alex's bad side, they will have to start planning their funeral.

"I plan on going with some friends of mine and just having fun with them." I try to say this as if it is nothing so that he will just move on in the conversation, but it doesn't work. He rolls his eyes at me with a teasing smile, as if I am being silly.

"C'mon, a gorgeous girl like you has probably

been asked by a ton of guys, so tell me which one you said yes to." I want to groan and tell him that I wasn't lying to him, but a person appears at my side that makes this whole situation with Alex much worse.

"Hi Colomba, how are you?" Luis says as he appears at my side, a joyful grin on his face as he looks down at me. His eyes glance up to see who I am walking beside, and the grin instantly disappears. "Alex." Luis states without emotion, although a slight growl can be heard in his voice. Alex glares at Luis with only slightly controlled hatred.

"Louie." Alex states in the same emotionless tone Luis had just used, but his voice has clear menace hidden behind it. The two of them stare at each other above my head, Alex glaring with pure venom while Luis stares at him without any feeling, as if Luis is staring at nothing important, which I think is making Alex even more angry. They stay like this, in a silence filled with fury before Alex finally breaks the tension. "So Louie, I was just talking to Colomba about who she is going to the dance with. She's trying to be cute and not tell me, you wouldn't know who it is would you?" Even though his words sound like they would be said in a friendly, teasing way, Alex growls each word with loathing in every syllable. For some reason, it feels like Alex is trying to see if Luis is going with me. Alex has thought of Luis as competition for my attention before, apparently he thinks Luis is his competition to become my boyfriend too. Luis does not get intimidated by him though; he keeps the same straight face as he responds.

"She isn't trying to be cute Alex, she really isn't going with anyone. She's coming along with *me* and a few of our other friends. We will have a great time hanging out together." Luis seems to be challenging Alex with his tone, and Alex meets his challenge head on by asking one last question though.

"Well oops, I had thought she was trying to hide that she was going with someone else. I would have been surprised if she said that she was going with you, wouldn't that just be crazy of her to take *you* to the dance?" My hands clench into fists at my side while Luis' calm stare turns into a very controlled glare. He doesn't answer Alex's question, but instead speaks to him in a calm, yet annoyed voice.

"Bye Alex. Colomba and I need to get to our next class, and we don't want to be late, isn't that right Colomba?" I look up at Luis and smile at him gratefully, so happy that he is helping me get out of this stupid, uncomfortable situation.

"Yes, that's right. We have a test today that I really don't want to be late for. Bye Alex." I wave at Alex as Luis and I start walking in the opposite direction. Behind us I can hear Alex saying his farewell.

"I'll see you later Colomba, I'll need to talk to you about something very important. And I will see you later too Luis." That last sentence almost sounded like a threat to Luis. It sends a shiver down my spine, and I am too afraid to look back and see if Alex is following us and too afraid to respond to him, so I just keep walking next to Luis. Glancing up at Luis I think about how happy I am that he is here beside me to help. I'm still a little shook by Alex's behavior, and having Luis by my side just makes me feel safe and secure. He is such a good guy.

"Can you believe that guy? What a creep." Luis grumbles as I see the knuckles of his fist turning white in his anger. His anger suddenly fades as he looks down at me with concern in his eyes. "You will stay away from him, right? He seemed pretty hostile, and I don't want him messing with you." I smile up at him, trying to be reassuring. Luis is so sweet to worry about me like this.

"I'm going to try my best to avoid him. He has been really annoying about asking me to the dance. He acts as if I am already his girlfriend and I'm being rude by not saying yes. I wish that he would just leave me alone so I can have fun at the dance. It was awful how he was practically interrogating you. That guy just seems crazy now."

"Yeah, he just really doesn't want to lose to me." Luis smirks at his comment while I become confused by it.

"What do you mean lose to you?" A deep blush forms on his cheeks and he instantly tries to avoid eye contact.

"Well I- I mean- umm. He always seems to think that I am trying to be with you, so he thinks of it like a contest of me against him with you as the prize I- I guess." He says all of this in a rush, while he becomes uncomfortable and nervous as his face turns red in embarrassment. I can't help it, I giggle at him.

"That guy is such an idiot, to think that I have to be won over is so dumb. Even if it was a contest, I would never pick someone like him as the winner. I would have to be brain dead to want to be with him.

Besides, you and I have been friends for a long time, if we liked each other like that, we would have been dating already by now." Luis chuckles softly at that comment.

"Yeah, we would have." Luis appears to be feeling awkward again and I'm not sure why. Did I just make him feel bad by something I said?

I think about what he said about Alex thinking about Luis as competition for me, and my mind immediately goes back to last year on Valentine's Day. On that day, the Crow created his latest victim, a girl who could make people fall in love. She made me and Luis fall in love with each other. We apologized to each other after it was all done, but sometimes it still feels like something is wrong. It's as if the spell hasn't completely worn off between Luis and me. I can see it whenever situations like this pop up. Just like with all these other situations I am facing right now, I have no idea what to do about it.

The two of us walk in silence until we get to our next class. There is a tense feeling in the air of the classroom, just like there always is whenever we are about to take a test, especially a big test like this. I know that I studied and that I am ready for this test, but I am still very nervous. Everyone looks pretty nervous too, some more than others though. One guy is sitting in his desk near the back of the classroom, and he looks like he is about to pass out from the stress. I have seen this guy around before, but this is the first class that I have ever had with this guy. Even in a small-town school like this, I can still manage to not have someone in my class by my Junior year even though there's only around a hundred people in my class. That may sound like a lot of people, but for a class of high schoolers, that's not much.

This guy is called Rick and right now he looks like he is so stressed that he is going to throw up. His skin is starting to become dripping with sweat, and I can see a panicked look in his dark eyes. His hands are fidgeting on his desk, as if he is unable to hold still. His eyes dart around the room as if he is scared that someone will notice how nervous he looks. I quickly look away before he can see that I was looking at him, I don't want him to feel embarrassed. I know that he gets made fun of a lot because of his nervousness, and I don't want him to feel like I am doing that to him too. This guy, Rick, is actually pretty well known at my school, but not for good reasons, it seems that everyone makes fun of him, even some of the other kids who get bullied. I am interrupted in my thoughts of Rick as the teacher tells us to sit down so that we can start on our tests.

Luis and I sit as the teacher starts passing out the exam. Taking out my pencil, I start on the test, my pencil is flying across the paper as I make my way through the first section of multiple-choice questions. Glancing up for a moment I can see that everyone else in the class seems to be moving a bit slower through the test than I have. Some people are looking down at their papers as if they want to just sink down through the floor and disappear. Luis even looks a little frustrated, but he is still getting through the questions, which is better than a lot of the people in the class who are just sitting there staring at the paper. A strange sound from the back of the classroom makes everyone slowly turn to stare at where the sound is coming from.

Sitting in his desk, shaking like a leaf, is Rick. The sound he is making is kind of haunting. He is wheezing slightly as he tries to breath while tears stream down his face. His hands are clenching and unclenching on his desk while he keeps his eyes down on his desk, trying to ignore all the people who are now staring at him. I turn away to focus back on my test, knowing what is going on and not wanting to embarrass him. Rick has things called panic attacks every once in a while when he is really stressed or afraid. I'm guessing that he feels very stressed now because of this test. I know that when he has these attacks he is embarrassed since everyone stares at him like he's being weird, so I try to ignore it when it happens. It is a completely normal thing, it isn't like he is having a serious medical problem, but everyone treats it like it is a strange thing, like he's a freak. I can already hear a few people chuckling at him as the final minutes of the class are being spent.

"What's the matter Ricky, you scared?" I hear one of the guys tease him mercilessly as a few people chuckle at his cruel remark. From the corner of my eye, I can see that there are still some people staring at Rick while the teacher sits back and does nothing. Rick glares at a guy, who I guess was the one who teased him, before he takes his test paper and quickly writes down some answers to his test. From how fast he is writing, I don't think he is really thinking about the answers and is just writing whatever comes to mind. There is a sinking feeling in my gut that, since he rushed through the test, he is probably not going to do well. He walks up to the teacher's desk, handing over his test paper.

"I'm done, can I go to the library please?" The teacher can see the distress in his face and can obviously see what has been happening so the teacher lets him go. An angry thought runs through my mind that she should have stopped the other kids from laughing at him, but at least she gave him the small mercy of being able to get out of the room. I can just tell that he wants to go so that he can avoid everyone who saw him having his attack. As soon as he is out the door, a few people snicker, and I hear one person talk about how Rick is "such a coward" and that he is "such a baby". I want to tell them off and say that he has a condition that gives him those attacks, he is not any of those things that they are saying, but we are in the middle of a test, and we aren't supposed to be talking.

Glancing back down at my test, I try to focus on the questions, but all I can hear are people continuing to make fun of Rick and his most recent attack. They snicker at him and mimic the wheezing sound that he had made. Thankfully, it doesn't take me long to finish my test and I ask the teacher if I can go to the library as well. The teacher agrees and I head out of the classroom and down the silent hallway, hoping that I can find Rick in there so I can see if he is alright. It takes a few minutes of walking to get to the library, but when I open the doors into the peaceful room, I can already tell that he is not in here. Groaning softly in disappointment, I sit down on one of the comfy chairs in the reading area and pull out the book I am currently reading as well as my cell phone. I open my phone to have a quick look at it to see that Rick's attack is already up on A-Streamer, someone had apparently been filming it when it happened. The comments under the video are all making fun of him for being a wimp, a chicken, as well as so many other insults that make my blood boil at the sight of them. I close my phone and pick up my book to read, trying to get rid of the image of Rick's pain filled face. I try, but I do not succeed.

Chapter Four
Luis-
The Video

As I finish washing my hands in the guy's bathroom, a notification on my phone chimes, breaking the silence of the lonely room. Pulling it out of my pocket, I look at it to see that it is a notification from A-Streamer. Clicking on it, I am immediately shown a video. In it I see a repeat of what I saw in class earlier, Rick having his panic attack. I end the video as soon as I recognize what it is, feeling disgusted that someone was so cruel that they would film that and then put it up online. Doesn't anyone have any kind of decency in this world? Can't people see how cruel they are being? Don't they realize how much this will hurt Rick if he saw it? Why can't people just be kind for once in their lives?

I shake my head realizing that I am being stupid asking those questions. Of course they don't, they don't care, they don't care about anyone but themselves. These disgraces of human beings just want to put other people down so that they can feel better about themselves. I dry my hands with a paper towel before walking out the door to get back to class. Rick is kind of like me, picked on for something he can't control. He has to face all this ridicule while having to deal with mental health problems alone while the world wants to beat him down for his problems. It isn't fair, but then again, this is life, when has life ever been fair?

After I saw Rick have a panic attack for the first time a few years ago in middle school I looked up what panic attacks are and how it affects a person, and I must say that I'm very sad that Rick, let alone anyone, has to deal with it.

A lot of people who have a panic attack for the first time go to the hospital because they think that they are having a heart attack, which apparently feels very similar to each other. Your chest tightens and it can feel very painful, you tremble uncontrollably, your heart races like you just ran a few miles, you can have trouble breathing, and you can feel very weak and dizzy. Most people get these if they have some kind of anxiety disorder or are going through a lot of stress. Considering the fact that Rick has been having these for a very long time, he probably has some kind of anxiety disorder. I wouldn't know for certain though since I am not real close with him, and I doubt he would tell someone he barely knows about his mental health. These attacks usually happen when a person is under a lot of stress, but can also happen randomly for those who have bad anxiety disorders. That honestly sounds like the scariest part to me, to have one of those attacks happen just out of the blue. That would be awful, not to mention embarrassing. I can't imagine what Rick is going through right now, but I know it probably sucks. Imagine having enough stress that your entire body just starts freaking out. I can't think of anything that could make me so anxious that my body would do that, but from what I have seen with Rick, it could be many things that people deal with all the time. I have seen him have panic attacks during tests, presenting things in front of the class, and even talking to people. I wonder what could cause me to be so frightened that I would have an attack like that?

Just my luck, I am instantly given an answer to my question when I turn a corner and I almost bump into one person that I know could make me that afraid. Alex is walking with one of his football buddies on either side of him. Alex was showing them something on his phone before he noticed me, but now he smirks at me as if he is a little kid who just found a new toy to play with.

"Well look who's here boys," Alex chuckles to his friends and they softly laugh along with him, sensing what he is about to do. I think I am sensing it too, but I know I can't run, they will easily catch me. "Did you see this yet Louie?" Alex shows me his phone so that he can play the video of Rick having his panic attack. "You know Halloween is coming up Louie? I wonder how much I will have to scare you to get you to act like that?" Without any warning, Alex shoots his fist forward, heading directly for my face. I quickly jerk to get out of the way, but Alex stops only an inch from my nose. His friends start laughing at me while I feel my face growing red in embarrassment for falling for his stupid prank. Alex shakes his head, pretending to be disappointed. "Oh well, didn't work this time. I guess I'll have to try again harder. See you later Louie." Alex moves around me so that he can walk past, but his fist swings downward and hits me straight in the gut as he walks by. Alex laughs loudly as a wave of pain flows through me with such force that I bend in half at the waist in agony. My stomach hurts so bad that I'm afraid that I'm going to throw up. "Well, at least that one worked." Alex laughs like the sick, twisted idiot that he is as he walks down the hall with his friends. One of them laughs with him, but one of them doesn't. He looks back at me for a moment with pity and then looks at Alex as if he is both surprised and scared by what he just saw. He is only like this for a fraction of a second though before he starts to uncomfortably laugh along with them. I recognize this guy. He is a freshman and just got on the team, he may have felt truly bad for me, and may have been scared of what Alex did, but I could see what the struggle was that was going on in his head. Should I stand up for how I feel and say that was a terrible thing to do, or will I be accepted by the team I just got on and keep the friends I just made? He obviously made his choice, and because of that I am now in pain and am alone in the hallway.

After so much experience with getting beat up by Alex I recognize the feeling in my legs and I know that they are about to give out due to the pain, I lean against the wall and let myself slide gently to the ground in a sitting position. I stay there for a minute, trying to get my breath back. Looking down the empty hallway where Alex and his friends went, I think about what Alex had said. He said that it is close to Halloween, and he wants to see how scared he can make me. I chuckle softly through my deep breaths as I think about how much I might scare him instead. Maybe he will be the one to feel true fear.

Chapter Five
Colomba-
The Day Before
Halloween

Halloween may be tomorrow, but it seems that a few people are trying to start the fun a little early. Throughout the day, I have seen people in masks jumping out and scaring people before running off before any teachers could catch them and get them into trouble. Someone in a weird mask that looks almost like the face of a giant spider almost scared the life out of Nat. She almost ran down the hall in her fear before I grabbed her so that she could see that it was only a guy in a mask. I wanted to punch that guy in the nose for scaring Nat like that, I didn't, but I surely gave him a piece of my mind. By the end of my five-minute rant to the guy he apologized to Nat, looking very guilty. At that moment he looked like a little kid who just got scolded by their mother. I guess, in a way, I was probably acting like a mother to that guy for scolding him like that. Oh well, he needed to hear it.

Right now, Nat and I are walking down the hall to get to our next class while she tells me about the costume she plans on wearing for the Halloween dance tomorrow night.

"And there is a fake parrot on my shoulder that can speak if I push a little button on his feet. I am going to be the best pirate you have ever seen." I chuckle at her excitement.

"I bet you will be considering I've never seen a pirate before." Nat rolls her eyes at me playfully.

"Okay, yeah sure Birdy, whatever." The two of us laugh with each other for a moment before I stop dead in my tracks and I immediately stop laughing, my demeanor suddenly becoming very serious.

Hiding behind a corner are three guys, three very large guys each wearing a letterman jacket for the football team. Even though they are all wearing frightening looking Halloween masks I can tell who the leader is. Behind the mask of a werewolf with blood going down its fangs is Alex. I can tell that it is him behind the mask based on his figure, he looks far more muscled than anyone else on the team.

The three are crouched behind a corner, every few seconds glancing around the corner to see who is coming. They seem to be searching for the right person to scare. My heart leaps a little in my chest when I see Rick coming down the hall, and when Alex looks around the corner and sees him, he seems to perk up in excitement. Alex quickly whispers to his friends, and I know what has happened. They have found their perfect prey for their mean little prank. I start marching over towards Alex, my hands balled into fists at my side in my anger.

"Alex, stop!" I yell this out to him, but Alex just ignores me as he and his two friends jump out from around the corner and scream at Rick. Rick drops his books in his surprise and leaps back, his fists raised as if he was afraid that he was going to be attacked. His entire body is quivering in terror while everyone in the hallway laughs at him besides Nat and me.

As the crowd stands still to laugh at him, I move through them to try and get to Rick. As I get closer to Rick, I notice something strange that makes me instantly worried. He is still shaking and his breathing is starting to become ragged as the shaking gets worse. His eyes look frightened as he looks at the people laughing around him. It only takes me a second to figure out what is going on and I start moving faster to get to him. He is starting to have another panic attack due to the scare and the embarrassment he now feels. I need to get him out of here and fast before they start trying to make things worse for him. My hope is shattered when Alex takes off his mask, staring at Rick with excitement, I can tell that he has already figured out what I saw, his panic attack is coming.

"Hey, look at this everyone! What is it Ricky? You going to freak out again like the freaking spaz you are? You going to cry like the pathetic little worthless, cowardly worm that you are!?" Everyone starts laughing again as Rick's breathing becomes more uneven and starts sounding more like a wheeze. My rage finally boils over, and I yell out loud enough for everyone to hear me.

"Alex!" The hallway falls silent at my one word. Everyone is too surprised that someone has the guts to stand up to Alex to say anything. The crowd parts for me so that I can get to Alex and Rick more easily. I stand in between Alex and Rick, my hands on my hips as I stare up at Alex with venom.

"What is wrong with you, can't you see that he isn't feeling well? You are making him feel worse!" Alex chuckles at me and opens his mouth to say something, but he is beaten to the punch.

"Shut up Colomba!" I turn around in a flash while Alex glowers behind me at Rick who is glaring at me, hatred and embarrassment in his eyes. "I don't need your help so stop butting in! I don't need *anyone's* help!" The fierceness in his voice makes me back up a step, almost bumping into Alex. Alex must have thought that since I moved closer to him in fear, I wanted his protection since he wraps one arm around my shoulder in a protective gesture while his other hand flies forward and punches Rick in the face. Rick falls backward, his hand going to his face to catch the blood oozing from his nose. He looks down at his bloodied hand, up at Alex's rage filled face, and then at the crowd of people around him who are also glaring at him with anger because he yelled at me. A bit of fear passes over Rick's face before he rushes to get back onto his feet and runs off before Alex can try to do anything else to him. Squirming out of Alex's grip, I start running after Rick.

"Rick wait!" I feel a large hand grab hold of my small wrist, stopping me in my tracks. Glancing back, I see that it is Alex holding me back. He looks at me with his usual confident smirk, usually I just see this as his normal expression, but today it makes me shake with rage.

"C'mon Colomba, don't bother with that guy. Why don't you come with me, and I can take you to your next class while we discuss your plans for the Halloween dance. Maybe we can turn your plans into *our* plans." Everything I have felt within the past few crazy minutes crashes over me within a second as my free hand swings forward and slaps Alex across the face. I did not use my full strength, so it probably didn't hurt a big guy like Alex that much, but it startles him enough that he backs away and lets go of my hand. The entire hallways falls deathly silent in their shock that I would have the guts to do something like that to Alex. Since everyone is silent, they can all clearly hear what I have to say to him.

"How on earth can you say something so cruel Alex? Don't you know that a lot of people have those kinds of attacks because something bad has happened to them in the past? They go through something traumatic and it changes them on the inside. You could be making fun of someone who has already suffered enough. You should be ashamed of yourself. I would never go to any dance with *anyone* who would do something so heartless." I march through the crowd trying to catch up to Rick. With the big head start he had on me though, it is practically impossible, I can't even see him anymore. I stop in the middle of the hall as the crowd around Alex starts to head to their next classes. I give myself a moment to hang my head in despair before I head to my own class too. I may feel terrible that I failed to help Rick, but I can't let that get in the way of me getting to class. I hurry to get there and make it just in time before the bell rings.

Sitting down at my desk, I can see from the corners of my eyes that there are people looking at me and whispering to their friends. I can tell from the looks they are giving me that they are talking about what just happened between me, Alex, and Rick. Judging from how shocked everyone was, I am going to guess that they are mostly talking about what I did to Alex. I bury my face in my hands at the thought of it. Honestly, I feel a bit ashamed of that now. Alex lashed out at Rick and punched him in the face because he insulted me, Alex let his emotions get the better of him, and then I slapped Alex because I let my emotions get the better of me. I am no better than him. I have never done anything like that before. What is wrong with me? I suppose that I have just been frustrated for a while now and it just built up until that happened. Glancing out the window, I see something that instantly reminds me of what has been frustrating me for so long. A crow sits on the branch of a tree outside as it makes a nest for itself.

My thoughts instantly go to the Crow and what my grandmother said about him and me. The two of us are supposed to be in love? Ridiculous. I can feel my hands clenching into fists on my lap at the idea of such an unbelievably irritating thing like that happening. I could never love someone like him, I could never love a monster. Glancing back up at the little bird, I feel my fists loosen as I let myself relax. I can't let my anger get the better of me, not again. I need to let go of this rage or else I will do something mean like what I did to Alex.

As I wait for the teacher to start class, I try to think of ways I can apologize to Alex as I hear the whispers from the other students as they tell everyone about what I did.

Chapter Six
Luis-
Halloween

The day has come, Halloween. A day full of candy, costumes, parties, and just a ton of fun. For me though, today means something different, today is all about horror and vengeance. Colomba doesn't know it, but I saw her try to defend Rick from Alex yesterday. I will admit that the part I loved the most about it was her slapping Alex across the face. That memory will be forever cemented as one of the most beautiful things I have ever seen, Colomba is definitely the most beautiful though, no contest. The look on Alex's face was priceless, the most hilarious shocked and in pain face I have ever seen, it looked as if his entire heart was being ripped apart. Knowing that the girl he liked was angry enough to hit him even though he knows that she is one of the least violent people ever was probably painful enough to make even a guy like him regret his actions. Hopefully, now he can take a hint and stop bothering her since it is obvious that she doesn't like him.

Another important thing that happened then

though was Rick and how he felt. He was in distress and Alex and all those people around Rick laughed at him, pushing him even farther. They were turning his problem into a joke. In his eyes I saw pain, so much pain that he lashed out at Colomba with rage even though she was trying to help him. I will admit I still feel pretty angry about how he spoke to her, I almost wanted to lash out at him too. It took a lot of thinking last night, but I decided that I will still grant him some mercy and give him the powers he needs so that he can get his revenge. When he is under my spell, I may even teach him a few manners when it comes to speaking to ladies, especially ladies as kind as Colomba. I will have so much to teach him, like how he might be able to get his revenge on all of these horrible people who would make fun of him for having a problem like that. I'm sure that will be a very fun lesson for him to learn.

Before the first class starts, I wander down the hall to find Rick. It honestly isn't difficult. It isn't hard to find someone if a bunch of people are laughing at them. From down the hall, I watch as people laugh as Rick walks down the hall while people make snide remarks about the video someone put online about his panic attack the other day. Rick's eyes are narrowed in fury, but he remains quiet as the world seems to laugh at him. The anger I see is beautiful, I know that he is ready for me.

The first bell rings, signaling that the first class is about to start. Everyone rushes to their classrooms, while I head to the bathroom. Opening the door, I scan the room to see that it is empty. Placing my hand over the Crow Medal, Shadow instantly appears, perched on top of one of the stall doors.

"Hello Master, how are you today? Do you need me to help you manipulate anyone's emotions today or are we sticking to the usual give powers, have them fight Silver Dove, and then lose plan?" Shadow says all of this in a very cold tone, and I know that when she talks about manipulating emotions she is referring to when I made Colomba fall in love with me with the Flying Ace. She is still pretty mad at me for doing that, I'm mad at myself too, but I'm not willing to talk about that right now, I have a mission to complete.

"None of that today Shadow, transform me into the Crow, I have work to do." Shadow merely sighs in response to that before she hops off the top of the stall and flies around me faster and faster until she is a black blur. I close and open my eyes again to look in the bathroom mirror to see the Crow staring back at me. The Crow smiles and looks absolutely evil in that moment, I find joy in it. The smile quickly disappears though when I hear something, my head snaps to the side to see the door to the bathroom opening. My heart pounds in terror as I realize my fatal mistake, I forgot to lock the door.

The door opens to reveal a guy I don't really know. He stops in his tracks the instant he sees me standing in front of the mirror. The two of us just stare at each other, him looking at me with a very strange look on his face that I can't really recognize while I stare at him in fear, wondering what he is going to do and what he is thinking. That moment of terror shatters when the guy scoffs at me and walks into the bathroom.

"Aren't you a little old to be wearing Halloween costumes to school?" My heart stops as I realize that I am safe, this idiot thinks that I'm just some random kid in a costume. I smile at the guy, and I notice him slightly flinch at the sight of it.

"You might say that." I use the same deep tone of voice that I use whenever I am the Crow, and the guy shudders a little before chuckling softly.

"You may be an idiot for wearing a costume like that to school, but you sure got the character right, I can give you that. Good luck trying to not get beat up wearing that costume." The guy goes into one of the stalls while I wait at the counter until he exits. He is noticeably confused when he opens the stall door to see that I'm still here, but he just washes his hands in silence before heading out the door, and I follow him a moment later to lock the door this time. I laugh softly before I get down to business.

"Shadow, find Rick." I watch through Shadow's eyes as she makes her way through the hallways, turning around corners and finally flying straight through a closed door so that she can find him. He is sitting at his desk, his face close to his paper as he writes, obviously trying to distract himself from the people whispering at him, asking him when he's going to freak out again. Shadow enters his hate filled heart and I speak to him.

Rick. Rick practically jumps in his chair in surprise, making the people around him laugh. He doesn't even feel bothered to notice this though, he is too afraid. His heart pounds like crazy as he tries to figure out what is going on. In the back of his mind, he is wondering if he will have another panic attack for people to make fun of him for just because of an imaginary voice in his head. You will walk out of this classroom right now so that you can receive your orders. A good soldier needs to follow the commands of their leader, especially one as unforgiving as the Crow.

I didn't think it was possible, but his heart races even faster as he asks the teacher to be excused and then quickly rushes out of the room while a few people chuckle about his strange behavior. As soon as he is in the hallway, I speak to him again.

Good Rick, very good. I like it when I have a soldier who follows orders as soon as they are given. I think that you and I will work very well together.

"What do you want from me?" he whispers out loud even though there is nobody else in the hallway to hear him.

Isn't it obvious Rick, I'm here to help you. They tease you about something you can't control, they tease you for your fear. Today is Halloween though, a day of fear. Perhaps you should let them share your pain. Perhaps you should show them what true fear really is. What do you say?

Rick doesn't have the usual hesitation that I see whenever I try to transform someone. As soon as I started talking to him, he started thinking about all of the people he wants to get back at, the people who try to scare him and give him another panic attack. He wants to make them feel enough fear that they could have a panic attack too. He wants them to feel all of the pain and horror he has been facing in his life.

"Okay Crow, I'm ready. Give me this power and I will make the world fear us." I chuckle to myself as I think that this has to be the quickest time I've had to convince someone to give them powers. It almost feels as if Rick has been waiting for something like this to happen for a very long time, then again, he has probably been bullied for this problem for a very long time.

Shadow invades his hate filled heart and spreads throughout his body like a virus. Rick does not seem frightened as he feels this happen, in fact, he laughs. Rick laughs as he feels Shadow taking him over. The laughter grows louder and louder until it echoes down the hallway like something you would hear in a horror movie. It doesn't take long for the transformation to be complete, when it is done he stands in the hall, breathing hard in his excitement. The creature that was once Rick is ready for vengeance. I feel his excitement grow as he looks down at what had once been his hands. A dark, sinister chuckle forms in his throat that quickly changes into a booming laugh that echoes down the halls in a way that even makes *my* skin crawl. When I hear that laugh, I know that he was telling me the truth, he will make the world fear him and I am excited to see him do it.

Chapter Seven
Colomba-
The Monster

At the front of the classroom, the teacher is trying to start the lesson while a little more mischief than usual is going on around me with the other students. A few people came to school in costume, and those are the ones who are causing a bit more trouble than most. These people are trying to distract the other people who are trying to pay attention by doing little pranks like taking their pencils off their desks when their attention is elsewhere so that they think their pencil is missing or trying to sneakily place things in the other person's backpack. I know that it is just a bunch of harmless pranks, but it is kind of annoying and rude that they are doing this while the teacher is talking and when these other people are trying to pay attention to what she is trying to say.

I try to ignore them the best I can so that I can pay attention, but it is very difficult. My attention is suddenly taken away from the teacher as a dark feeling comes over me. A sudden shiver goes down my spine and a sinking feeling in the pit of my stomach tells me that something is wrong, something is about to happen. This is the feeling I always have when one of the Crow's little slaves tries to do anything, or when anything really bad is about to happen. Within the classroom I am sitting in, everything seems alright when I glance around the place, everyone is just looking down at their work or doing little pranks. I close my eyes so that I can focus my attention on what I can hear. Within the classroom there is nothing but the sounds of pencils scratching across paper and the other students making little sounds here and there while the teacher goes on with the lesson. The lights suddenly go out, leaving the room in a faint light from the windows. Everyone starts looking around to see who is the one doing this prank, but nobody steps up as the prankster. While they are distracted by this, thinking that it is something as simple as a prank, I have a sense that things are about to get so much worse. One sound from outside the room does catch my attention though, the sound of something sliding across the floor. Something very big, something moving very fast, and something coming right towards my classroom.

Before I can scream out a warning to everyone, screams of terror can be heard outside the classroom. Everyone looks at the door while some stand up as if they are about to head out of the room to investigate. Nobody has the opportunity to do this though. Before anyone can react, a massive object smashes through the wall and then lands on the ground, sending rubble flying in the air in a massive cloud of rocks and dust.

Everyone scrambles to the opposite side of the room, trying to get away from this thing, but I notice this too late, and I see that they all moved away from the door and are now cornered against the back wall. I stand in the middle of the room alone, too terrified to move as I watch the object that had crashed through the wall get up slowly as if it is a living thing. As it lifts itself, I can see that there is more of this object still in the hall, so it is very long as well as very big. It is shaped like a large tube as wide as a doorway with one end of it kind of circular, the size of a small car, that is the part that is slowly lifting into the air that everyone is watching. It is black in color, and covered in the dust and rubble from when it crashed in. When the creature has lifted one end into the air at least eight feet, it shakes itself, getting the rubble off it and then opening what I finally realize are two eyes, two blood red eyes. It opens a wide, horrific mouth into what looks like the twisted smile of a demonic clown. Two large fangs around the length of my arm are displayed as soon as it opens its mouth. A thin tongue with a forked end slithers out of the mouth between the teeth, almost as if the creature is trying to wave at all of us with its tongue. When that mouth is open, I realize what I am facing, I am only a few feet away from the largest snake in the whole world, a snake big enough to crush a firetruck within its grasp. As that thought hits me, my entire body starts to quiver when I realize that it could kill me without barely even trying and yet I haven't even moved away from it yet. I am too paralyzed by fear to move. That doesn't seem to be a problem that the other's share though, as soon as the rest of the room figures out what we are facing they all scream in fear at the monstrosity in front of us. The creature joins us in the noise as it opens its fang filled mouth and releases a roar that eerily sounds similar to the sound dinosaurs make in the movies.

With the noise of the screaming and roar of the monster, it feels as if my ears are going to explode. When the roaring ends, the entire room bursts into frenzied movement. The students and teacher run around to try and find another way to exit the room since the creature is blocking the doorway. A few people try to open the window, but it won't budge. One guy solves that problem as he throws a chair at the window, shattering it into countless pieces. Everyone tries to get out as fast as they can without scratching themselves on the broken glass. While they are all scrambling in their fear, I remain where I am as I just stare up at the creature, my fear fading away. Everyone else may be scared and confused, but I am not anymore. I am a little frightened, but not confused at all. I see this for what it is, another trick by the Crow. So what power did he give this person? The ability to create hallucinations? The ability to be a giant snake? What? What could it be? And who is this horrible creature?

The creature seems confused by how calm I am since it lowers its head so that it can look into my face. The snake puts its face only a foot or so away from mine, either to intimidate me or it can't see well and has to be this close to make out my face. The blood red eyes stare right into me, making me feel as if that creature can look straight into my soul. I can feel the snake's breath brush against my skin, blowing my hair back past my shoulders. The two of us stand there together, both of us deeply confused by each other. We stare, wondering what is going on in the other's head, me wondering who this is and why the Crow gave them powers, while they are wondering why I am not afraid like everyone else and why I am standing here in front of a giant snake. We stay like this for a minute before the creature swiftly turns around and slithers down the hall. Screams from other students down the hall follow the creature while I am still standing in the same spot. What on earth just happened?

Okay, I have no time to think about this, I have work to do. I need to find a place to transform into Silver Dove and stop it before it harms anybody. I have no idea why it didn't hurt me, maybe it's like some creatures in movies where if you don't move it can't see you, or something like that. I don't know why, but it must be stopped.

Rushing into the hallway, I am almost run over by a crowd of students running in terror like a stampede of cows. I quickly start running with the crowd to not be run over and to also run away from whatever it is that is scaring them. Behind me I can see the snake again, slithering madly as it turns its head to the different people running around it, trying to get away.

A few people try to open the doors leading outside, but they are barricaded from the outside with a bunch of desks and other furniture. I'm guessing this is either the work of this creature, or the Crow got his shadow dogs to do it while everyone was still in class. The people who had been trying to get out quickly realize that it is a losing battle and start running again with everyone else. I take a glance behind me to see that the vicious snake is still following, at least for a moment. The creature stops, turning its attention to something else.

Its crimson eyes stop on this one girl who is stuck in a corner of lockers, her back to the wall as she stares up at the creature. I run out of the crowd and run in the opposite direction, heading towards the girl and the giant snake. Everyone else might be too afraid to do something, but I am not.

As I run towards them, I blink my eyes, and within a millisecond, the creature has changed its form. The massive serpent is long gone and has been replaced by a clown the size of a regular human. Most aspects of him are normal, all except his mouth. The red paint around his mouth looks more like blood and it is dripping off of the creature's chin. Sharp teeth smile cruelly at the girl who runs down the hall, crying in her fear. She cries as if she is facing her worst nightmare. The creature stays behind, letting a cold, haunting laugh follow her down the hall as she runs and screams for help, but I don't think anybody will help her. Everyone is too terrified to help anybody, and I am too in shock to move. When the demon clown is done laughing, he follows after the girl, giggling like a maniac.

What just happened? Did the Crow make this person into a shape shifter? That could cause a lot of trouble. One thought stops me in my tracks though. That girl looked as if she was facing her worst fear when that thing turned into that demon clown. It is almost as if that creature can turn into what you fear the most, that would make a lot of sense for the Crow to do on Halloween, it would be very fitting for the holiday. Interesting to know that the Crow is being festive with this. Kind of a weird thought.

I'm about to separate from everyone and find an empty place to transform when a familiar face practically runs into me. I jump back in surprise, but instantly calm down when I recognize the person.

"Nat! Man am I glad to see you, we need to get out of here! Did you see the monster the Crow has created now?! It seems to turn into what people are afraid of or something!" Nat is breathing hard as sweat pours down her face. I don't know if she is sweating because she has been running around or because of the fear, either way she is soaked with it.

"I saw it, trust me, I saw that crazy thing and I don't want another look at it! Let's find a way out of here before it comes back!" A crashing sound comes from the right and the two of us turn to see that we are the two unluckiest girls in the world right now because the first thing we see is a guy from my English class running away from a giant rat the size of a truck. As the guy runs past us, the giant rat skids to a stop in front of Nat and me. It looks back and forth at the two of us as we stay frozen in our terror. Its gaze stops on Nat and I watch in horror as more legs sprout out of the rat's back, it loses all of its hair as it all just falls off the creature and onto the ground, and it's mouth morphs into a set of menacing pincers. Within a moment, the giant rat has changed into a spider so large that it almost touches the ceiling.

Nat doesn't need any more warning, she sprints away from the creature with me following not too far behind. As we run, I take a few glances back at the creature to see that we are at least keeping a little bit of a distance between us. In between deep breaths to keep myself running, I yell ahead at Nat.

"*Why*?!!! Why did your worst fear have to be spiders Nat?!!" She doesn't even look back at me as she responds.

"Because spiders are scary, that's why!!" If I wasn't so afraid I would have rolled my eyes at her.

"But you're so much bigger than a spider Nat!!"

"Yeah, tell that to this thing behind us!!!" She points back at the creature, and I cannot argue with her logic there. I quickly look behind us to see the most horrific thing I have ever seen. A spider as big as a truck is scurrying on its eight huge, hairy legs to get to us. Its eight black eyes glare at us looking like dark bowling balls stuck to its face. The giant spider's pincers are biting the air as if it is eagerly waiting to bite into Nat and I so it can eat us.

My legs push me farther and farther through the halls as the giant spider's spindly legs scurry behind us, while my mind races faster than the three of us put together. I need to get away from both of these guys so that I can transform into Silver Dove and stop it. As the three of us run, I see my opportunity. Up ahead, the hallway is splitting into two, whatever hall Nat goes down, I'll go down the opposite. Since the creature is currently transformed into Nat's biggest fear it will most likely follow her, leaving me alone. I feel a bit bad leaving Nat by herself while she is so frightened, but if I do this then I can save everyone. That is the sacrifice I must make.

When we hit the split in the hallway, Nat takes a

left and I go right while the spider chases after Nat. I breathe a sigh of relief as I start heading down the hall to try and find a quiet place to transform into Silver Dove. My head moves from side to side as I search for a place, but everywhere I look I see doors with people's faces poking out to see if the creature is approaching, no empty hiding spot free from peeking eyes in sight. I'm about to move further down the hall when something grabs my arm and I let out a little shriek of fear. I'm about to start running away when a familiar voice comes from behind me.

"Colomba, it's just me!" Glancing behind myself, I see that Alex has a hold on my arm in his large hand.

"Alex? What are you doing here?" He smiles down at me, trying to look confident even though I can see the fearful sweat on his skin.

"I came to find you beautiful. I felt that you needed some protection during all of this, so I have come to the rescue." Oh my gosh, why does this guy have the worst possible timing of anybody I have ever met? I want to roll my eyes at him and just run off to do what I need to do, but his grip on my arm is strong. I may be strong myself, but with him being so large and me being so small, it is no contest. As long as he has a hold of me, I am under his control.

"Alex-"

"Don't worry Colomba, I forgive you for what happened the other day when you slapped me. You were just upset, so I don't mind getting over it and protecting you now." Before I even have a chance to tell him to go away and that I don't want his protection, he grabs my hand and practically drags me down the hall, I'm guessing, in an attempt to get me to a safe place.

Great, now how on earth am I going to get out of this?

Chapter Eight
Luis-
My Monster

I order my monster to stop following Nat since I cannot stand seeing one of my friends so scared. I couldn't let him and anybody else figure out that I was trying to avoid her so I let him do it for a minute but then told him he should find a new victim to scare since he was already spending too much time with her anyway. If I had told him not to go after her and anybody realized that I was giving her special treatment, they may have realized that I am friends with her, and then it wouldn't take long for them to realize that I am the Crow.

He followed orders and turned into some horror movie alien monster when some guy passed him, and my monster started chasing him instead. This alien creature he is now has multiple tentacle like arms and legs that are really long that are apparently supposed to be used to grab the alien's victims so that it can eat them. I never watched the movie, so I don't know, but within my monster's mind I can see scenes from the movie playing out in his head, and from what I see I'm glad I've never seen it. It looks way too bloody and gross to me. I don't really like horror movies since I think that they are just too scary, kind of ironic considering what powers I gave my newest soldier. This is kind of the perfect power to give to my soldiers to be honest. If he can transform into whatever a person fears the most, then nobody will ever dare to cross him, and he can cause chaos as long as he wants. This is beautiful to see, seeing all the stupid people of my school running in fear of the person they were making fun of just yesterday, and that person they were making fun of is now chasing them down the hall as they practically pee their pants in terror. No matter how many times I create a new soldier, this is always my favorite part, seeing all of these cruel people finally getting what they deserve. It is the best feeling of revenge that I think anybody has ever had.

As my monster chases the guy, he makes a quick move and manages to hide beneath some desks and other stuff that had been placed in front of a door to a classroom, acting like a barricade. I'm guessing that some people put it up to keep the creature out and protect whoever is inside the classroom. The monster loses interest in the hiding person, it can sense other prey nearby that will be easier to get. He knows that they will be easy since they aren't even trying to stay quiet, they are talking loudly so that the creature can hear them even though the creature can't see them yet.

"C'mon Colomba I'll keep you safe and get you out of here." Wait, Colomba? She's about to face my creature again? And who is that guy she is with who's trying to protect her? I think I recognize the voice, but it is hard to tell since I can only hear him through the ears of my creature, it isn't as strong as if I was hearing it with my own ears. Only a moment after that guy spoke, I hear Colomba's sweet voice.

"Alex, let go, please. I don't need your help. I-I… I need to find Nat. So please just go on your own so I can find her." I can hear Alex scoff at her. Of course, a guy like Alex would want to use this opportunity to look like a hero to Colomba. Sadly, for him, and awesome for me, she doesn't seem that impressed. In fact, she sounds pretty annoyed with him. I'm guessing he has been dragging her along for a little bit now. My creature stays still as it waits, it can hear them coming from around the corner and it wants to shock them by seemingly just silently appearing from nowhere.

As soon as the two come into the creature's eyesight my monster springs into action. I watch as the massive alien changes with a speed I didn't think was possible. Within a moment, the tentacle- like legs got sucked back into the body, the alien shrunk, and the colors seemed to blend together like a massive ball of paint until the thing is made up of completely different colors. I hold back a gasp of shock as I see someone that I recognize in the thing that just transformed. I have only seen this person a few times very briefly, but there is one day I have seen him that has been stuck in my head ever since. It was after a football game and Alex's dad screamed at Alex since his team didn't win, he treated Alex like dirt. That is who stands in front of Alex now, his father, or at least an illusion of his father. The only difference though is that this illusion of Alex's dad has glowing red eyes, like a monster in a movie. A low growl, like an angry dog, seems to come from the illusion of Alex's father, making Alex look away from Colomba due to his curiosity.

"What are you looking at you pathetic little weakling?!" The illusion of Alex's dad screams. Alex's eyes grow wide with absolute terror when he sees who is in front of him and he drops Colomba's hand in surprise. She takes the opportunity to run the opposite direction, but Alex is too surprised to notice. Alex opens his mouth as if to speak, but no sound comes out. It is obvious that he is too terrified to be able to say anything. The illusion of Alex's father shows his impatience as he yells in a growling voice, *"Well, speak you spineless little insect!!!!"*

"Dad, what are you doing here?" Alex asks, barely above a whisper. The illusion glares at him with its demonic red eyes. I can actually see Alex shivering in his fear.

"What am I doing? What are you doing?! Why are you just standing there, shivering like a worthless, cowardly worm?! You need to do better than this Alex! I'm so disgraced to call you my son! Any son of mine should do better than this! Yet here you are doing nothing like you always do! Go out there and make yourself stronger so that the world won't step on you! I'm not surprised if the world already does! Bugs like you deserve to be stepped on!" As he says that last sentence his voice turned far more menacing with a horrific growl in it, as if a lion somehow learned how to talk. Alex stumbles backward at the sound of that growling voice. He

lands on his butt, but doesn't stay there long, he scrambles back up to his feet and runs away. A young man runs away from his father as if he is running from a monster.

As the creature watches Alex running away, it laughs evilly, taking joy from his fear. The menacing laugh of Alex's father chases after him as Alex runs away in terror. I, on the other hand, do not laugh. I can't laugh, not at something like that. My hands hang heavily at my side as I just watch the world through my monster's eyes with a pained numbness. Even though I can still see the world, my mind is filled only with the image of Alex's horror filled face when seeing his father. What have I done?

When I decided to give Rick the power to become what someone fears the most, I expected him to just turn into the usual stuff people say they are afraid of like spiders, monsters, and bears or something like that. I didn't think about how some people might be afraid of something a bit more sad than that. I never expected to see someone afraid of their own father. My heart is heavy as I am overrun by guilt. I have seen how Alex's father acts around him, I can't believe I made it even worse just now.

I shake my head, trying to get rid of these thoughts. This *is* Alex we are talking about, a monster like him doesn't deserve my guilt or sympathy. Even though I say that in my mind, the image of his horrified face stays in my mind. I need to do something right now to get my spirits up again. Down the hall, I see something that brings a smile to my face.

Take a look down the hall my friend, I

believe you will find a new plaything to have fun with.

My monster glances to the side to see a lone figure walking toward it, constantly looking around themselves to make sure that nothing is following them. Since my monster currently looks like another human, Angela has no fear of him, so she keeps coming closer, not really noticing us. My creature smiles wickedly as he starts moving carefully towards Angela, trying not to gain her attention.

As Angela continues to glance around the hallway in panic, the creature sneaks up behind her and transforms silently within an instant. As soon as Angela has turned around, the creature now looks exactly like Angela's father, the mayor. I can tell it is him due to his greying hair, nice suit, and handsome face, the perfect looking small-town politician. I have no idea what is going on here. Why is Angela afraid of her father? It usually looks like she is bossing him around to get him to pay for stuff, she wouldn't do that if she was afraid of him. I have no idea what's about to happen, but I'm sure it will be interesting. Angela's eyes grow wide at the sight of her father.

"Daddy, what are you doing here?" Angela's fake father looks sad with his head lowered, and he looks like he's about to cry at any minute.

"I'm so sorry, my little princess, I'm so sorry. I have made a terrible mistake in our family business and I have lost everything!" Angela's eyes grow wide with horror while I burst out laughing. "I'm sorry, my princess, but you will have to sell all of your nice clothes and purses so that we can afford food. We will also have to move out of our mansion and into a small apartment so we can afford the bills. I'm so sorry princess, but you will also need to get a job so that we can support ourselves. We will need the extra money, I spoke to a friend and they said you can get a job flipping burgers at the diner downtown. You will probably get yelled at and treated like dirt by the customers, some may even be your classmates, but you will have to go through with it so that we can survive." Angela screams in her frustration, fury, and terror as she drops to her knees, face in her hands, as she bursts into tears.

The creature wanders off to seek out a new victim, leaving her crying on the hallway floor while I am in the bathroom, my stomach hurting a little because I am laughing so hard. That definitely put me in a better mood. My creature wanders down the hall, searching for a new victim while my dark mood slowly disappears as I think about all of the cruel people he gets to scare to make them understand his pain.

Chapter Nine
Colomba-
My Fear

My heart pounds as I run, my body is already getting worn out. I have been running for what feels like forever, trying to find a quiet place to transform into Silver Dove, but whenever I go in some room or closet there is someone already hiding in there. How can I save everyone if I can't have the privacy to transform? If I keep up all this running, I'm going to be too tired to fight this creature, but I have to keep going, I need to save the school.

I'm starting to feel more and more desperate as I go down hallway after hallway, finding no place that I can hide. As I go down yet another hallway, I am frozen in fear as a girl screams, sprinting down the hall in terror as a shark swims through the air like water, chasing after her, snapping its teeth as if it wants to eat her. The girl manages to run far enough away from the creature that it loses interest in her and just starts to swim slowly through the air, its head turning from side to side with its beady red eyes searching every corner it can see, obviously trying to find its next victim.

Slowly, I move away from the creature, being careful not to make any noise so that it won't notice me. I have almost reached the entrance to another hallway, almost reached safety, when something happens that sends a chill down my spine.

Apparently, I wasn't the only one trying to escape the creature, but unlike me, this person didn't care about making noise. From behind me, someone ran out of their hiding spot and accidently knocked over the janitor's mop as they went. The mop seems to fall in slow motion as it drops to the floor, creating a horrible clattering sound that echoes down the hall. I turn back around to see that the illusion of the ferocious shark is glaring down the dark hall directly at me with its demonic glowing red eyes. The illusion sucks all of its fins back into itself and it swirls together just like it is mixing together ingredients to make cookies. It looks like one giant colored mass with strange things floating in it. The huge mass of color quickly changes, losing its color until it is practically only black. Within a moment, the creature changes itself into the form of the Crow. I feel myself jump back a little in terror at seeing my worst enemy. My horror only gets worse when I see that this fake Crow is standing in front of the bodies of several of my friends as well as my family. Right beneath his feet are Nat and Luis. My heart, which had been pounding from all the running a moment ago, is now practically screaming as it races faster than it ever has before. I am so terrified that it feels like I am about to have a heart attack at any second.

It takes a moment of silent horror before I realize

something strange, the creature appears nervous. It looks down at itself, seeing who it has become, but afraid to play the part. I instantly understand why, it is nervous about what its boss, the real Crow, would think about its little act. Instead of doing anything, the pretend Crow just looks at me. I can see it quivering slightly in its terror, afraid of what the Crow will do to it.

As it is frozen with fear, I run away from it, racing down the hall as if my life depends on it. My feet carry me several hallways away before I finally enter the library and hide amongst the bookshelves. It is very dark in here, and I hide in between two shelves so that I can catch my breath while still being hidden. Looking around, I can see that the library is actually empty. That's a bit surprising, but I don't have time to think about it. I need to use this moment to transform, there is a monster that needs to be fought. Placing my hand over my Silver Dove Pin, I get myself ready to fight.

Chapter Ten
Luis-
What She Fears

Through my monster's eyes, I watch as in a stunned silence as Colomba runs away from my creature, who looks just like me. My entire body feels numb as I see the girl of my dreams run away from her greatest fear, me. What have I done? I have made my best friend and the girl I love fear me. How could I have done this to such a sweet person as Colomba? How could I cause such a wonderful person so much fear? What kind of monster am I?

If I am to judge by what Colomba saw in this creature, I am the kind of monster who would kill the people she loves considering the image that was created from her fear is the Crow standing over the bodies of her loved ones. My stomach begins to ache as I feel my heart being crushed in my chest from the overwhelming grief I feel. I let out a few sobs as a couple of tears fall from my eyes and disappear underneath my mask. I have made myself a monster. I cannot escape this now, I am the monster.

I can tell that my creature is trying to pretend

that what just went down with Colomba never happened since he is now moving on and has found a new victim, he is now swimming through the air through the halls as a huge school of piranha fish chasing after a girl from my English class. He was probably trying to find a new victim as quick as possible so that he wouldn't be stuck looking like me a moment longer and possibly make me angry. That was probably a good idea on his part since I do feel very angry right now, but more than anything, I am depressed. I have made myself something terrifying for the girl I love and, despite everything in my mind telling me I shouldn't, I still feel terrible about what happened with Alex earlier with the illusion of his father. I need to get away from all this for a minute so that I can calm myself.

My creature, I am going to be walking in the halls, beware you will not recognize me as the Crow, but I will try to avoid you. I need to look over the damage we have created. I want to see our progress. My creature answers quickly, like a well trained soldier.

Yes Sir, I will continue on with our mission while you are away. Do not worry I will do my best. I almost want to chuckle about how serious he sounds even though he looks like a bunch of floating fish right now. It's kind of funny in a weird sort of way.

Good. Keep this in mind though, my

monster, I will still be keeping an eye on you even if I am not in my Crow form. If you mess up, I will see to it that your powers will be a thing of the past and they will not be given back under any circumstances. Do we understand each other?I can sense a bit of fear go through him at the thought of losing the powers he has already fallen in love with. He knows that without these powers, he is nothing and he never wants to be nothing again.

Of course Sir.

Closing my eyes, I let my powers fade so that I become myself again. With that done, I unlock the bathroom door and take a peek outside. When I see that nobody else is there, I step outside and quickly wander through the halls, seeing the devastation my creature has made. Entire walls have been knocked down by my creature, the remains of those walls are scattered in chunks of rock all over the floor. Abandoned backpacks and other school supplies are spread all over. Despite the signs of destruction, it is disturbingly silent, it is so quiet that the sound of my breathing seems to echo down the halls. My footsteps sound more like a giant dropping boulders within the quiet halls as I make my way to the front of the school. I want to be at the front of the school because that's the last place that my creature saw Colomba. I need to find her, I need to make sure that she's alright. It looked like she was making her way to the library from what I could see through my monster's eyes so I will check there first.

While I walk, I try to think about what I can say to her, but nothing comes to mind. All I can really think about is the look of fear on her face when she saw my monster turn into me. As the image of her frightened eyes looks straight into my soul, I realize that there isn't anything I can say. I am a monster.

I know that I can comfort her as Luis, but I can never get her to forgive me as the Crow. If you are someone's literal worst nightmare, there is no forgiveness, you are cursed to be hated by them forever. I know that she will never love all of me, after everything I have done.

Turning a corner, I find myself in the large entry room of the school. The row of doors leading to the school's front lawn are only twenty yards from me, but standing in between them and me is a tiger the size of a truck. I jump back a little in surprise before I realize the obvious, it is only my monster trying to scare someone else. It definitely worked too since the person he was scaring runs screaming past me. The tiger had kept its eyes on its prey, so it now has a perfect view of me. My heart stops in my chest as the tiger's eyes look straight into mine and its lips pull up into a demonic smile as it shows off all of its massive teeth. I feel its terrible joy as it realizes that it has a new piece of prey to play with. The orange and black stripes of the tiger seem to melt together into a mass of many colors swirling frantically. Its limbs and body changes shape like he is made out of clay. Within the span of a second the colors form into a new creature, one that causes my stopped heart to start beating at a record pace.

Standing in front of me is a dog the size of a car.

Its ink black fur stands on end as it growls menacingly at me. It lowers its massive head as it makes its way slowly toward me, as if it is preparing to lunge at me. Its massive paws are as big as dinner plates, and they walk toward me steadily as it pulls its ears back, its red eyes glowing like fire. It looks a lot like the dog that bit me when I was a little kid. Because of that dumb dog, I'm now terrified of all dogs, and it is also why I made my shadow creatures look like dogs as well. This dog looks like it should be guarding the gates to the underworld, not here at my school, yet here it is as real as can be.

I know that this is only my creation, it isn't a real monster dog, but I am still too terrified to move. What is wrong with me? Why am I so terrified and not running away even if I know that this is fake? The dog snarls as it slowly moves closer to me while my feet remain planted to the floor. I am about to start speaking to my monster through his mind to tell him to not attack me, but I can't. If I tell him not to attack me then he might figure out who I really am and then somebody will finally know my secret. I can't let that happen. If I can't do that then what am I going to do? Thankfully, I don't have to answer that question myself, I get a little help.

A small figure moves so fast through the air that they look like just a silver blur. My monster is thrown to the other side of the entryway, crashing into a display case full of sports team trophies. The display case shatters; glass and now dented trophies scatter across the floor with a crash and clatter. My monster whimpers as his black tail goes between his legs as he looks back in fear at the spot he was standing in only moments before. Someone else stands there now, Silver Dove.

"Aww what a cute little puppy." Silver Dove mocks my creature using a little baby-talk voice. "But I think this little puppy needs some obedience training, he's being very naughty." My monster's fear instantly disappears as his ears flatten on top of his head and his lips pull up to reveal his menacing fangs. A furious growl leaves his throat as he lunges towards Silver Dove, but she lunges toward him as well. The massive dog opens his mouth wide to bite at her, but she grabs hold of his upper and lower jaw, keeping them pried open, only inches away from biting down on her head. Silver Dove turns her head toward me, panic in her gaze beneath the mask.

"Run!!! Get out of here while I've got him!!!" She groans a little as she pushes her arms forward, pushing the monstrous dog away from her. For the only time ever, I am happy to take Silver Dove's advice. I sprint across the entryway and open the door to the principal's office, hiding behind the principal's secretary's desk so that I can watch and see what happens. As I see the demonic dog start trying to circle Silver Dove to try to find a weak spot, I think to myself that this is going to be one incredible fight.

Chapter Eleven
Colomba-
The Fearful Monster

The stinking, hot breath of the monster dog seems to fog the air around me as I try to dodge its dagger like teeth as it tries to bite me. From the corner of my eye, I had seen Luis run off into the principal's office, safe from harm. Thank goodness. I want to breathe a sigh of relief for that, but I am a little too busy trying to not get munched on by a crazy giant demon dog. When his jaws snap right in front of me for what feels like the billionth time, now that I know Luis is out of the way, I swing my fist forward and hit the mutt right in the snout. My strike sends the pooch flying across the school's entryway and right through the doors leading into the library. The doors are crushed under the massive beast's weight, smashing them into little splinters of wood and glass.

The dog rolls off of its side and back onto its feet in a matter of seconds. It growls furiously in its embarrassment, its teeth are bared at me, warning me that it will attack again. The rumbling growl seems to echo through the entire school, but it's probably only within the entryway. It lowers its head as it starts moving forward, the sharp claws on its black paws clicking against the tile of the floor. The jaws of the creature open wide, and I expect it to bark or roar at me, but instead I am greeted by the angry voice of a young man.

"If you keep getting in my way Silver Dove, I will make you regret it! I will make everyone feel my fear, and you will not stop me! I will make them regret everything!!" He scrapes his claws along the tile in his anger, causing a horrible screeching sound that sends a shiver down my spine, but his words also give me a shiver as well. 'Feel my fear'? What on earth is that supposed to mean? What does he mean by 'my' fear? Who is this guy that the Crow has transformed and why does he want to scare everyone so much?

The dog lunges at me again, its mouth opened wide so that he can try to use me as a chew toy. I step to the side so that he misses me, but I did not expect his reflexes to be so good. As soon as he saw that he missed, he snapped his head backwards and snapped his jaw right on one of my wings. I only have a split second where I feel the teeth tighten their grip around my feathers before he yanks me backward, sending me tumbling to the ground in my surprise. The air in my lungs gets forced out of me from the impact and I cough a few times as my body tries to get more air again. A massive paw steps on top of me so that the massive dog is right on top of me, his heavy paw forcing me down. I stare straight into the face of the horrible creature, its teeth smiling down at me as it feels victorious. A slimy bit of drool hangs from the massive dog's mouth and drips onto my face. I grimace as the warm slime falls in the opening of my mask and lands on my nose. Oh my gosh this is so gross, I almost feel like puking. I want to wipe it off of my face, but if I make any sudden movements then the creature might try to strike at me in this vulnerable position. I need to be careful with my next move. The creature laughs when he sees that I am momentarily beaten.

"The great and powerful Silver Dove, taken down by little old me. That's just hilarious." The dog lets out a booming bark of a laugh, throwing its head back as it did so, almost like it was howling like the dog he is. He looks down at me again, a thoughtful expression coming over his face. "Hmm, I think I should end this fight in a new form, I've used this one a bit too long. I want a special form to take you out, but which one should I use?" His eyes light up as a brilliant idea seems to flash through his mind. "I have the perfect idea, a form that everyone fears. I've always been afraid of the unknown, it triggers me to not know what's going to happen. I guess that's what everyone is afraid of, things they don't understand. That is what all humans fear, I'm glad that you will be the one that I can show this to. Maybe you should feel honored that you have the privilege to see this."

The huge dog stands up on its hind legs, releasing me from its grip, as it slowly begins to transform right in front of my eyes. Black tentacles, dripping with black sludge sprout from the dog's flesh as the skin on the dog's snout peels back to reveal its skeleton with flames instead of eyes glaring down at me, the fury in the fiery eyes clearly shows its hatred within the skeleton's eye sockets. The fur on its tail quickly sheds off to reveal a snake that starts snapping its jaws as soon as it is revealed. I watch in horror as the creature's body changes shape with the sounds of snapping bones and stretching flesh as the body looks more like a furry, giant human's body instead of a massive dog's. The monster throws its head back, opening up its skeletal jaws to shoot fire out of its mouth like a dragon.

I stare up at it with wide eyed awe and terror. What on earth am I going to do now?

Chapter Twelve
Luis-
A Defeated Monster

My heart feels like it is about to explode in my chest it is beating so hard. I am looking out of the principal's office into the entryway, looking at the most horrifying thing I have ever seen in my life. Out of everything he has transformed into today, this has to be the most terrifying. It looks like I am viewing something out of the worst nightmare possible. Even with my big imagination, I couldn't think of anything this creepy. I actually feel a bit bad for Silver Dove right now since the creature is still above her as she lies on the ground looking up at it with a look of true fear on her masked face. The creature laughs at her terror.

"Pretty terrible isn't it?" The monsters asks with a devilish growling chuckle. "I have always hated how my fear is so much more noticeable than others, it is good to see the fear on everyone else's faces for a change." A spark of realization seems to come to Silver Dove, and I barely hear her whisper a single word from where I am hiding.

"Rick?" That stops the creature from laughing. It growls as it picks Silver Dove up by the front of her armor, holding her up to his eye level, about ten feet off the ground. I can see her eyes grow wide as she looks into the flame eyes stuck in the eye sockets of the dog skull.

"How dare you call me that!" The beast roars in her face. "I am Fear, I have no other name anymore. Fear is all that I am."

"Really? Is that going to make you happy, just scaring people all the time?" Silver Dove growls sarcastically. This annoys the creature even more, and he throws her across the room, but she is prepared this time. She opens up her snow white wings to catch herself in the air and she starts flying a few feet off the ground. The creature goes down on all fours, his claws digging into the tiles on the floor before he charges at her like a wild animal. When he gets close to her, he lifts one of his massive paws to swipe his huge claws down the front of her, but she blocks that by holding one arm above her head. Her remaining arm shoots forward and punches him right in his skeletal face. The creature lets out a loud whimper as he falls backwards and rolls a few times from the strength of her strike. When he stops rolling, he turns his head towards her, growling furiously while his snake tail snaps at her. Silver Dove takes the opportunity of this moment to speak again, this time though, she is not so sarcastic.

"Rick, please listen to me. The Crow just gave you these powers so you could hurt people, so you could be the bad guy. You aren't a bad guy Rick, you shouldn't let yourself do something like this. You are better than this." The creature gets back onto all fours again while he chuckles at her.

"Who says I am? I don't believe so. They all made me like this. They all hated me and always tried to get me to have a panic attack to watch me be in pain. They loved giving me fear, so I let myself become the villain so that I could do the same to them. I'm giving them a taste of their own medicine, an eye for an eye. They deserve it." Silver Dove doesn't waste a second, she responds to him instantly before he can say anything more.

"Yeah, but an eye for an eye makes the whole world blind. Yes, what they did to you was wrong, but that doesn't mean that you have to scare them too. You have an anxiety disorder, that doesn't give you the right to make everyone else afraid or nervous. Just because you have an issue doesn't mean everyone should share your pain." The creature releases a roar that makes the glass on the windows vibrate as he charges at her again. With a movement so fast I didn't even notice it, Silver Dove had taken out her sword as she moved out of the way and sliced off the snake tail of the creature as he passed her. The snake falls to the ground, twitching and hissing for a minute before it goes still and disappears into a bit of smoke, disappearing into the air like the nothingness it always was. My monster sees this, and he steps back a bit in surprise. He does not let it bother him for too long though, he glances back at the nub that was his tail and within a moment a new snake has appeared there, but one that is much bigger than before. It looks like the king of all cobras. My monster chuckles when the snake begins to snap and hiss at Silver Dove again.

"You cannot defeat me Silver Dove, I can just keep coming back no matter what you do. I have grown strong by feeding on the fear of everyone in this school, I am feeding off yours right now. I can feel the fear coming off you this very second, you fear me." I see fire forming through his skeletal fangs and I know what's coming. "Just as you should." The monster shoots fire from his mouth at her like a dragon and she dodges out of the way at the last second, flying through the air with her sword drawn. My creature seems to have expected this though since he swings his body around so that his snake tail can have a chance to get revenge. The snake bites onto Silver Dove's armor, latching itself on, before it reels her in like a fish on a fishing pole. It pulls her in so that she can be face to face with the monster. All the fight seems to leave Silver Dove when she looks into his eyes because her sword just hangs down at her side, her arm limp as she stares at the creature, breathing hard from the fight. The creature laughs softly and menacingly in her face, enjoying the look of defeat on her.

"The brave and mighty Silver Dove, taken down by Fear itself." He chuckles again. "How fitting that I am the one to defeat you. All the others before that the Crow gave powers to were weak, but I knew what I needed to defeat you. Fear makes everyone weak, so I needed what would make you weak, your terror. Fear makes even the strongest person turn into a sniveling little baby and because of that I have finally won! The Crow has finally won!" My heart begins to pound in my chest in excitement as I realize that he is right. I did it. I finally won. I have defeated Silver Dove! I can't believe that this is happening! After working on this for over two years I have finally won! My moment of excitement and joy is broken though when, in the silence around me, I hear someone softly laughing. I look closer at my monster and Silver Dove to see that Silver Dove is laughing in my monster's grip. My monster starts growling at her, but this still doesn't stop her. She only stops laughing to speak to him.

"That's ridiculous. Fear isn't a weakness. Don't you see, fear is something we need, sometimes fear is what makes people good." The monster cocks its head to the side in confusion, so Silver Dove continues. "Fear makes people act better, they do not do bad things like steal from others because they are afraid of the consequences even if they really wanted what the other person has. Fear can cause a person to work harder, they are afraid of losing their dream, so they work hard so they won't have to live with the pain of failing. Fear can also make you afraid of ending up like someone who is bad, so you do everything in your power to change that. You are afraid of things, that is normal, and it makes you human, you just can't let the fear control your life. If you are constantly afraid that you will have another panic attack, then you will work yourself up so much that you will have them more often. You need to focus on the positive things in your life that will help you feel better. Whenever I am nervous, I work out to make myself feel better, you need to find your own ways of coping or else you will doom yourself into continuing down this path you hate. I can help you, but I can't make you do anything, you have to help yourself." The creature just growls at her words as he moves her closer to his enraged face so that she is only inches from his skeletal animal snout.

"And how can I fix this problem anyway? I've been trying for years without any luck! I gave up years ago because nothing was working, so how on earth can I fix it?!" Even though the monster is growling right in her face, she smiles at him comfortingly as she rests her hand on his skeletal face. The growling stops instantly at the feeling of that soothing gesture.

"It won't be easy, I know this Rick, but you must find a way. I cannot tell you how you can help yourself cope, because everyone is different, but I'm sure that we can find a way. I promise you that I will try my best to help you in any way I can, you just have to trust me." The creature looks thoughtful for a moment, like he's thinking about what she is saying. I'm about to yell at him in his mind to stop, but I do not need to, he suddenly becomes serious again as he glares at her.

"*Liar!!*" Using his snake tail that's still holding onto her, he throws Silver Dove through a wall and into the gym, creating a hold in the brick wall. The creature follows after her, smashing through wall and creating an even bigger hole. The fight is now out of my sight so, gathering all my courage, I leave the safety of the principal's office to run toward the hole they made to watch the fight continue. When I crouch behind the entrance to the hole, I'm surprised that I don't hear the sounds of fighting. Glancing into the hole in the wall, I see something surprising.

Silver Dove is standing in the center of the gym, looking at my creature, but the monster isn't looking at Silver Dove. My monster is instead looking at this one girl who had apparently been hiding in the gym during all of the chaos. Tears are streaming down the girl's face as she wheezes for breath. She is curled up in the fetal position on the floor, her body shivering violently in her terror. I recognize what is happening right now since I have seen Rick go through it before, she is having a panic attack. She must have been so frightened by what has been happening, and then these two came crashing through the wall just put her over the edge until she had the attack.

My monster stares at her with absolute horror. He slowly walks toward her, obviously trying not to frighten her. He is walking so quietly, and the girl has her eyes closed in her terror, so she doesn't notice that he is so close to her until he has his massive paw wrapped around her, trying to comfort her. When she feels his touch, she tries to scream, but she can't through the wheezing and sobs. My monster quickly moves his paw off of her as he lowers his head, looking ashamed at the sight of her fear.

"It's okay." The monster says, trying to help her feel better, but his menacing, growling voice just makes her sob even harder. "I'm sorry. Please, I want to help you." My monster begs her. He looks down at her sobbing figure, and then looks over to Silver Dove who is calmly watching the scene in front of her. The two just look at each other for a moment before Silver Dove gives him a simple nod and he seems to know what she means since he closes his eyes and before I can give him another order in his mind, I watch him transform from a hideous monster into Rick. The truth is simple to figure out, he gave up the power I gave him.

Rick wraps his arms around the girl in a tight hug, rubbing her back in a soothing way. He softly shushes her like I've seen people do with sobbing children before he speaks so gently to her that I can barely hear from my distance.

"It's okay, I know how this feels, but I promise you that you aren't dying, it may feel like it, but you aren't. You will be okay. This won't last much longer if you just let it happen. I'm right here for you. Nothing will hurt you, I'll make sure of that. I'll stay with you until it is all over, I promise." The girl's sobbing starts to calm down a little at his words. Glancing over at Silver Dove, I can see her smiling at Rick, looking proud of what he has done. Silently, she backs away and places her hand over the dove symbol and whispers something to herself as she begins to glow.

I know what is going to happen based on all the times I have seen Silver Dove in action, she is going to repair everything with that magic power of hers, but I don't want to be around for that. I want to be alone for right now. I felt victory for only a moment before it was taken from me, but that is not why I am truly upset. My heart seems to clench a little in pain when I think of that girl being in such terror that she had a panic attack because of what I created. My shoes drag across the floor as a bright light travels throughout the school, fixing everything. I hear countless teachers and students cheering, knowing that Silver Dove has defeated my monster, but I cannot feel happy right now. A huge boulder of guilt is trapped in my heart after what I have done today, and I know that it will take a while for me to be able to feel better about all of this. I have done too much.

Chapter Thirteen
Colomba-
The Aftermath

I glance out of the door to the storage closet that I am hiding in to make sure that nobody can see me. I just transformed back into my regular form in this closet, and I don't want anybody wondering why Silver Dove went into the closet, but Colomba came out. I have enough on my hands, I don't need anybody to find out my secret identity and make it worse. Knowing my luck, the Crow would find out and he would do anything he could to get back at me for every single time that I have defeated him.

When I see that nobody is around, I walk out of the closet and start walking down the hallway. The principal had announced to the school that everything is alright, that the Crow had been defeated, and that they can come out from their hiding spots so that they can go home, but nobody is coming out. My heart sinks in my chest as I realize why. They are too scared, the monster the Crow had created did what he had set out to do. He terrified everyone to the point that they are now too afraid to come out of their hiding spot even though they have been told that they are safe. They are like frightened rabbits hiding in their holes in the ground, frightened of everything that moves outside of their hiding spot. I walk all the way across the school to my locker before I see another person have the guts to come out of their hiding place. The guy is shaking all over, as if he is super cold, but I know that's not the truth, he is still terrified by everything that happened. Apparently some others must have been looking to see if anybody else would come out, and when they saw me and this guy, they decided that it is safe enough.

People walk out of the rooms, slowly and cautiously. They are looking around themselves as if they believe that something could pop out and attack them at any second. I guess after what happened today they should expect that. They are all shivering just like that other guy, their eyes wide with shock, and their skin pale, as if they had all the blood taken from their face. Like Nonna would say, they look like they've seen a ghost. Perhaps a few of them did since the monster could transform into what you fear the most. I can easily see that I am the calmest one in the hallway, I lower my head, trying not to look at anyone so that they won't notice that I'm not scared like them. If they notice that I'm not scared like everyone else, then they might get suspicious of me, and I can't let that happen. The problem is that it's hard to pretend to be terrified of something you have already defeated.

We are all heading outside to either get on the

bus, to have someone pick them up, or to drive themselves home. Everyone shares the same horror filled gaze. Nobody knows how to handle what just happened, and honestly, neither do I. I feel both happy and disappointed with myself in how things turned out. I am glad that all that is over with, but I am disappointed that I wasn't the one to stop Rick from being the monster. I have always been able to stop whoever the Crow transformed, but not today. Instead, he didn't listen. He wanted to keep fighting me and frighten everyone, nothing I said worked. The only reason he stopped was because he saw that he caused a girl to have a panic attack. He saw that he was causing someone to have the same pain he did, and he felt guilty. He let his powers fade so that he could comfort her. I didn't even really need to do anything, he would have eventually found someone and caused them to have some kind of reaction like that and then he would have done the same thing. I know I should be happy, but I feel as if I failed. I'm supposed to be the hero here, but the bad guy was defeated by his own conscience. That doesn't really sound like super hero material to me.

My thoughts are interrupted though by a familiar voice that instantly brings a smile to my face.

"Hey Colomba!" I glance behind myself to see Luis running up to me.

"Hey Luis, how are you? Did you get hurt with all that going on with the monster?" He shakes his head at me.

"No, I'm all good, how about you?" I breathe a sigh of relief at that news.

"Thank goodness, I'm alright too. I was hiding in a closet the whole time. Thankfully that monster the Crow created didn't find me. I did see you though, you almost got cornered by that thing before Silver Dove saved you. That must have been terrifying." A sudden dark look has come over Luis' face that I don't really understand.

"She didn't need to do anything, I could have gotten out of that situation by myself." From the hate in his voice, I think I know what is going on now. Luis has always hated Silver Dove, and to be saved by the person he hates probably does not feel good. I feel a bit annoyed right now though. I just saved his life and he's going to be so ungrateful? That's terrible, I thought Luis was better than this. My heart feels a bit hurt knowing that my friend thinks so little of me even though I may have saved his life.

"How can you say that Luis?" I ask with a little bit of pain coming through my voice that I was unable to hide. From the corner of my eye, I can see Luis look down at me with concern. "She saves your life, and you say something like that? Silver Dove risks everything to help everyone, and saves your life, and you act so ungrateful? What is wrong with you?" At first, his eyes open wide with surprise at my harsh words, and then his head lowers when he sees the truth in my words, shame clouding his gaze.

"I'm sorry Colomba, you're right. She did save me. I was too scared to move, let alone fight the thing off or run away from it. I'm sorry for what I said, and I wish that I could thank her for what she did." The sadness in his gaze melts away the pain I felt in my heart, I rest my hand on his shoulder and he looks back up at me in surprise.

"I'm sure that wherever she is, she knows how grateful you are." I smile warmly at him, and he smiles sheepishly back at me. Since I can tell that he still feels a bit uncomfortable about the apology he just made, and the fact that I scolded him, I decide to change the subject. "Hopefully none of this craziness will get in the way of the Halloween dance tonight. I worked really hard on my costume, and I don't want it to go to waste." His sheepish smile fades into an honest grin.

"Yeah, from the way you talked about it, I'm sure it will be awesome. I bet the dance will still happen, I mean everyone already bought their tickets and the principal didn't say anything about canceling it during his announcement. Silver Dove got everything cleaned up with that weird power she has that makes everything go back to normal after the fights, so they don't really have a reason to stop it." My smile grows even bigger when I realize that he is right, and hope returns to me.

"Awesome, I can't wait to dance all night." I mischievously nudge him with my elbow. "So when are you going to tell me what your costume is? You've been keeping it a secret for way too long." He laughs, hearing the teasing tone in my voice, and he joins along with my teasing.

"Well I can't really tell you that. Why would I keep it a secret for so long just to spoil it at the last minute? That's just dumb." I lean into him, teasing him further.

"Aww, c'mon, not even a hint?" He chuckles at me, joy lighting up his eyes.

"Nope, can't do it. I refuse to give up the surprise." I pretend to pout at him.

"You're so mean." He winks at me.

"I can accept that." I giggle softly.

"You're so *very* mean." I look away from Luis to see that the other people around us are still silent and in shock. Everyone drags their feet across the floor, all sad and pale looking. Even though Luis and I are fine after all that happened today, everyone else is still terrified. The monster fulfilled the mission the Crow gave him, he put fear into the hearts of everyone in this school. The Crow may have lost today, but he still had some kind of victory.

Chapter Fourteen
Luis-
The Halloween
Dance

Walking into the school gym feels like walking into a weird dream tonight. Monsters, movie characters, strange creatures, and other unusual beings are walking around and eating some food that is laid out on a few tables at the end of the room. Tables are scattered around the room while one area near a DJ has been left empty so that some of these people in costumes can dance. Loud music echoes around the room while the other students chat with each other. I feel a little uncomfortable standing in here all alone, but I am waiting for Colomba to arrive and she should be here any minute. I probably should feel used to being alone since I have been alone practically all of my life, but today just makes me feel even more like a loser. Maybe it's because I am at a dance, an event where you are expected to be with other people? Or maybe it's just because I'm awkward and I'm in a big crowd? Who knows?

Sitting at a table with a girl is Rick, back to his

normal self, laughing and joking with the girl sitting beside him. At a closer glance, I can see that the girl he is with is the same girl he had helped with her panic attack when he was still my monster. Apparently, she has forgiven him for scaring her, and even agreed to come with him to this dance. They look very happy together. Within their gaze, I can see how filled with joy they are being with each other. I look away from Rick so that I won't be reminded of what he was doing earlier today.

Glancing around the gym at the other people around me, I notice something pretty interesting. There are two costumes that seem to be very popular among the other students. Scattered among the crowd are people dressed up as either the Crow or Silver Dove. Some of the costumes are pretty good too. I passed one guy who looked almost just like me as the Crow, it was like looking into a mirror, kinda creepy to be honest. Something that is a little strange about this situation is that those who are in the Crow and Silver Dove costumes are staying away from each other. People wearing Silver Dove costumes are hanging around each other, and the same for those wearing Crow costumes, but people dressed as Silver Dove are not letting themselves be near anybody wearing a Crow costume and vice versa. They glare at each other like they are on opposing sides in a war. I feel a little shocked when I realize that is true. They are on opposing sides. Those who are fans of Silver Dove dressed up like her while those who are my fans dressed up like me. Just from seeing the costumes, these people now know that they are supposed to hate each other. I had felt pretty good seeing people dressed as me only moments before, but now a sickening feeling has come over me. When I look at the hate in their eyes when they look at the people dressed as Silver Dove or me, I realize that I am responsible. I started this, I caused all of this hate.

Shadow told me ages ago that Silver Dove and I are meant to work together to bring some peace to the world. I have been trying to bring peace to the world my own way, by making everyone afraid to pick on each other, but it hasn't really seemed to have worked at all. Silver Dove has told me multiple times that I needed to join her, that we could team up and help people the way we are supposed to, but I never listened. Maybe what she said is true. Maybe I am the one who is wrong here. I'm the one who refused to team up with her, I have refused her help, I have caused so much destruction and pain, and, when I look at the people around me, I can see the anger and hate I have caused. Maybe this all needs to stop. Maybe I need to talk to Silver Dove again. Maybe things should be different. Maybe… I hear a sound nearby that snaps me out of my thoughts, and I turn my head to see what that sound is.

Looking at the door to the gym, I am immediately stunned by what I see. Walking through the door is the most beautiful sight I have ever seen. Colomba stands in the doorway wearing a long dark blue dress that makes her look like a medieval princess, which is obviously what she is going for with that costume since she is wearing a little tiara on her head. Her dark blue dress is embroidered with golden threads to create intricate designs of flowers growing on vines. Out of all the girls in the school,

Colomba is the only one who could actually pull off looking like a princess. To me, she is one.

Awkwardly clearing my throat, I walk up to the princess and bow to her teasingly. When she sees what I have done, Colomba giggles softly.

"Good evening fair princess, you look ravishing this evening." I say to her in the most posh voice I can, this just makes her giggle even more. I straighten up from my bow so that she can see the costume I have created. I am also wearing medieval style clothes, but the clothes of a royal gentleman. There is no mistaking what I am trying to be since a fake crown stands prominently on my head. When Colomba told me what she was going to dress as, I knew that I had to be what every princess like her deserves, a prince charming.

Colomba smiles at me with innocent joy that makes my legs feel like jelly.

"Good evening fair prince, you don't look half bad yourself." She winks at me playfully, while I act teasingly flattered.

"Oh my goodness, I don't know what to say. I am just so overcome with joy at the sound of your compliments oh fair princess." She shakes her head at me, with that joyful smile still on her face. As she does so, the lights grow a little more dim and a slow song starts to play. A lot of people leave the dancefloor while a few couples remain, slowly swaying in time to the music. I smile, all traces of teasing gone from my face and voice. "Would the fair princess care to have a dance?" I extend my hand out to her which she accepts with a beautiful smile. Leading her out to the dancefloor feels like I'm walking on a cloud. As soon as we are on the dancefloor, we pull each other close as we move gracefully to the sound of the soft music. The two of us seem to move perfectly with each other, as if we are meant to dance together. This has to be one of the happiest moments of my life, sadly the happiness doesn't last long though.

Within the crowd off the dancefloor, I notice a familiar face sitting at a table wearing the costume of a comic book villain, Alex. He is easy to notice since I can feel his rage fueled glare directed right at me. Jealousy burns behind his glare as he looks at me holding Colomba close. He wants so badly to be the one dancing with her, Colomba had told me about how many times he asked her to this dance, but she said no every single time. From the disappointment I can see beyond the jealousy, I can tell that he was hoping that she would change her mind and have at least one dance with him. That hope is destroyed though, watching me with her. He obviously thinks that this is a date, that I asked her out and she said yes to me instead of him. His confusion is clear, he is wondering how a girl like her would lower herself to be dancing with a guy like me. I am honestly wondering that myself, but I can't complain. I am dancing with the girl of my dreams, and she seems to be having just as much fun as I am. I try to feel the same joy I felt before I noticed Alex, but I can't.

As his hate filled eyes glare directly at me, I can feel no sense of satisfaction knowing that I have beaten him again in regards to having Colomba's attention. When I think about what happened earlier today, I can only feel sad for him. He is probably so desperate for her attention because she is the only person who doesn't want to be around him just for his popularity, good looks, and money. She is honestly friendly to him, while the rest of the world is fake to him, and his family is cruel. I cannot feel satisfaction knowing that he is miserable. I look away from him, not because I am afraid of his glare, but because I cannot stand seeing the pain hidden behind those eyes.

When I look into those sad eyes, I remember something from a very long time ago that I had forgotten over the years. It was back when we were both in Kindergarten, when Alex and I were still friends. It was the end of the school day, and we were waiting for his dad and my Uncle Diego to pick us up to go home. My uncle's car pulled in first and when Alex saw him smiling and waving at me, a sad look came over his face. At that time, I thought he was going to cry.

"I wish my dad was more like your uncle." I looked at him, very confused as to what he could mean. I thought about his dad and how rich he was, thinking Alex was nuts to think my poor uncle was better than him.

"What do you mean?" Alex looked uncomfortable for a moment, scuffing his shoe on the sidewalk and looking down at nothing in particular.

"Well your uncle is nice and he is never mean to you. He doesn't yell and when he asks you about how your day is he actually cares about the answer. You never seem to be afraid of him." I didn't really understand what he meant at the time, and my little kid brain got immediately distracted when I heard

Uncle Diego call my name and I ran over to him, eager to get away from school. I didn't really think about what Alex said after that, and by the next morning I had forgotten about it. Now that I know only a little bit about what goes on at Alex's home, I can't help but feel bad for the life Alex has been given. He has all the possessions he could ask for with the money his family has, but he doesn't have anyone who truly cares about him, and his own family seems to hate him. I can only imagine the pain he holds deep inside him. If he felt jealous of me when we were little kids, maybe that's why he decided to choose me as his favorite target to bully. Maybe his jealousy turned into anger, and then that anger turned into hate, so he decided to hurt the person he hated to make himself feel better. I suppose, in a sad sort of way, it makes sense. If there is someone you hate, you would want to get back at them and that is exactly what Alex has been doing all these years, even if I never deserved it.

As the slow song continues on with its peaceful melody, I hold Colomba close as I try to push Alex out of my mind. I throw away my hatred for the time being, feeling only pity for him at the moment. My mind empties itself of those depressing emotions so that I can focus on what is important, the amazing girl in my arms. I smile down at her tenderly as she smiles joyfully, watching her feet to make sure we don't step on each other. She has not noticed the rage coming from Alex's direction, and I won't let her. I won't let that sad little boy ruin this wonderful girl's fun. I joke and laugh with her as we glide across the dancefloor. We are in complete bliss, while someone only twenty feet away is sending so much fury our way that it feels like hot coals are being put down the back of my shirt. I ignore that though, how can I be upset when I have the girl of my dreams smiling in my arms?

When she directs that beautiful smile up at me as she giggles at a joke I made, my joy fades when I remember another expression she had on her face earlier today. At school today, she had a look of pure terror on her face. She was terrified at the sight of me, or at least an illusion of me. When my monster had transformed in front of her to look like me, she was absolutely frightened. I am what she fears the most. To her I am the scariest monster she can think of. I am her greatest fear and yet she dances with me in joy and lets me hold her in my arms. If she knew who I really am, would she ever come near me again, or could she find it in her heart to forgive me? I don't think I can ever figure out the answer to that question, but I know that I should try to explain myself to her. I need to tell her that I am not the one she needs to be afraid of. I know that I can't do that now, not as I am. She wouldn't listen to me if I talked to her the way I am now. Besides, I do not want to ruin this moment, I am enjoying having her in my arms like this. I never want this moment to end. I know that this night will not last forever though and the dance will end. For now though, I let myself enjoy being with the girl of my dreams because I can never tell when I will have another moment like this.

Chapter Fifteen
Colomba-
The Monster in
Front of Me

I feel exhausted from dancing for so long as I open the door to my room and walk towards my vanity table. I glance at myself in the mirror, not wanting to take off my beautiful dress yet. I had such a wonderful time today, getting to defeat the monster that the Crow created, going to the party tonight, and getting to dance with Luis. I think that last part was my favorite... Not because I like Luis like that or anything, but because I enjoyed dancing with my friend. Luis is a wonderful dancer after all, and the greatest friend a girl could ask for. As I am about to take off the little tiara on my head, I notice something from the corner of my eye that makes me freeze. A dark shape is sitting on my windowsill outside and is looking at me. It is too dark to see what it is, is it a large bird or something that just got stuck there? While my mind runs through what it could be, the creature suddenly seems to grow until it takes up the entire window. My blood runs cold when I realize what happened, the creature was crouched down, standing outside my window, but it is now standing up straight and with the large wings behind it I know exactly what it is. I whip around to see the dark creature, the Crow, opening my window and stepping inside my room.

I am too terrified to speak or scream out to my family for help, I can only stare in open mouthed horror as the Crow gets his whole body into my room and then stands in front of me, only a few feet remains in between us. His wings are spread out so that the tips of them are touching the opposite walls of my room. I can only imagine how strange this must look, a guy with bird wings and kind of looking like a demon standing in a dark room with a girl dressed like a princess. It probably looks like a scene from a fairy tale where the little princess is about to be kidnapped by the villain of the story. I can only pray that's not what he plans on doing, or that he hasn't figured out who I really am. If he knows that I am Silver Dove, then I am doomed, I don't have the time to transform before he can get me. The two of us just stand here for a moment looking at each other as if we are both trying to figure out what to do. After a moment or two he seems to have figured it out first since he is the one to break the cold silence.

"Good evening Colomba." I take in a deep breath at the sound of his words, I hadn't realized I had been holding my breath in my fear. His deep, intimidating voice sends a shiver down my spine.

"What do you want?" My voice comes out in a pathetic whimper that almost makes me cringe at the sound of it. He takes a step closer to me, his hand extended out to me. I take a step back and bump into my vanity table. He steps back and his hand wilts back toward him. The Crow lowers his head for a moment, as if he feels bad about frightening me. He clears his throat awkwardly before he tries to speak again.

"I'm sorry for coming into your room like this Colomba, especially at this late hour. I hope you can forgive me for this." What on earth is going on? Why is this guy being so polite to me? He's kind of the villain in our school, so why is he being nice? Those thoughts are erased from my mind when I remember how he saved me from the Sprinter and carried me to safety. This guy has more sides to him than just the villain. Even though I know this, I can't ignore the fact that he broke into my house and is in my room without permission, so he does not deserve any of my politeness back.

"Why are you here?" He rubs his hands together as if he is nervous. Why on earth is this super powerful guy so nervous around a girl that he thinks doesn't have any powers, and thus can't hurt him? I suddenly remember how I had thought that the Crow has a thing for me, this seems to be proving me right even more, that would explain why he looks so nervous that he might puke since he is talking to me.

"I- I just wanted to- to say that… that… I'm sorry." My eyes grow wide in shock at hearing those words coming from him. Did he actually just apologize to me? I thought that a guy like the Crow would never admit that he did something wrong, even if he knew it was wrong. "When I saw what my soldier turned into when he saw you, I couldn't believe that I would be the thing that you would fear the most. You would never believe how much that hurt me to see. I never want you to be afraid of me. I want you to think of me as… as a friend." He never wants me to be afraid of him, yet he breaks into my house in the middle of the night? I am having some doubts here, either that or this guy is an idiot who didn't think this through very well. I feel my hands ball into fists.

"A friend? Really? Why would I want to be friends with you after everything you have done?" My tone is harsh, and I can tell by the sudden drooping of his wings that I have hurt him, but I don't care, he needs to hear this. He needs to hear the truth about what I think of him. "How could I ever be friends with someone like you? Why would I ever care about someone who causes so much trouble and tries to hurt people? Your monster turned into you, not because I am afraid of you, but because I am afraid of the things you do. You transform people into creatures that try to hurt other people. You call so many of the people in our school monsters, but you are the only monster I see. You are the one causing real pain here." I can see the feathers on his wings bristling in his anger, but I don't stop, I can't stop. "Why would I want to care about a monster who hurts everyone? Unless you change, that is how I will always see you. You will always be the monster." His feathers stop bristling as they droop again.

"You- you really feel that way?" He sounds as if he is about to cry, I suddenly feel bad about my cruel words and I want to apologize, but I realize that I may be finally getting through to him, I may be helping him realize that he is being the villain. I might be convincing him to stop. Even though I feel bad that I am hurting him, I can't let my words be softer or kinder. I cannot spare his feelings because he needs to hear what he really is. I need to be cold and harsh so that he can finally understand.

"Yes. Yes I do. Practically everyone else does too. You are the monster in our school, just open your eyes and see this. How could you be anything else but the villain here?" He looks straight into my eyes. Behind his mask I can see dark, miserable eyes looking back at me, eyes that look like they are about to start crying. Strangely familiar eyes too… weird.

"I- I did all of this for you." I feel my eyes narrow with confusion I stare at him with wide eyes.

"What are you talking about?" He lowers his miserable eyes again to stare down at his feet.

"Everything I have done as the Crow has been for you. You were in everything I did. I wanted to make all the bullying at school stop just for you, so we could be together." Okay, now I'm even more confused… and pretty concerned.

"I still don't understand, what do you mean? What do you mean that this was all done for me? I don't get it." My voice sounds panicked, I'm mostly scared by his comment about us being together. I'm so creeped out right now.

"You were never supposed to see me as the monster. You were supposed to see me as the hero, the one trying to end the suffering, but you decided to cheer for Silver Dove instead and all of those idiots at school decided to keep acting like monsters to each other so I had to keep up the act as the Crow. It was never supposed to go on for this long, and it wasn't supposed to be like this." He takes in a deep breath and lets it out in a heavy sigh before he looks me straight in the eyes, completely dead serious. "I have always loved you Colomba, since the day I met you. I knew that you were the one for me as soon as I saw you. Other people may say that we aren't meant to be; you are smarter than me, kinder than me, beautiful, and everyone loves you while everyone just views me like a bug. You may think the same way right now about me as the Crow and about me in real life, but I will prove to you that I deserve your love. One day you will love me just as much as I love you. I did all of this so that you would love me instead of viewing me as something less than human like everyone else." He looks out the window at the full moon, melancholy shining in his eyes. "I wish I could have told you this as my real self, but you would never accept me. A girl like you would never accept someone like me." Swallowing the fear in my heart, I step closer to him.

"Who says I would?" He looks up to stare into my eyes, hope suddenly shining in his gaze. I know that I was just insulting him a minute ago, but he has been revealing so much to me right now, if I could get him to feel some hope, he might actually reveal who he really is. When I find that out then I can figure out how to end this. He has said that he knows me and has had a huge crush on me, so I must know who he is. Once he takes off that mask, I will know how to reason with him based on who he is. "You say that I would never care for you, but I don't even know who you are. If you tell me who you are and how you feel, then I might feel the same way." He stares at me as if he can't believe the words he is hearing.

"Do- do you really mean that Colomba?" He comes up to me, holding his arms out to me as if he wants to embrace me but is afraid to.

"Yes, just try and maybe things will be okay. Just be brave and trust that I will help you. You know me, you know that I will try my best to help you. I don't want you to be this miserable since you obviously feel so badly about yourself. I want you to be happy. You trust me, don't you?" He laughs softly as if he is in absolute shock, yet feels absolute bliss. I see a tear fall from his eye and slip down his mask as a huge smile lights up his face.

"You- you really would, wouldn't you?" He steps closer to me until his outstretched hands touch my arms. It takes all my self-control to not flinch at the feeling of his fingers. I look him in the eyes, scared out of my mind, but trying to remain calm so that I can still convince him.

"Yes, yes I would. Please let me help you." His smile somehow gets even bigger, making me even more freaked out. It is so weird seeing the guy who has been the symbol of darkness to me for years suddenly smile at me. I am really disturbed right now and nothing in the universe will make this moment okay.

"Of course you would." The Crow practically whispers this to himself as if he has suddenly realized something obvious. He pulls me in close as he wraps his arms around me in a gentle embrace. Even his large wings curl in around me, as if he wants to trap me in his arms. Alright, I was wrong, nothing in the universe can make ***THIS*** moment okay. My heart is pounding in my chest in my panic as I try to hold as still as possible. His arms are holding me gently, but it feels like his arms are a cage around me. I have the strongest urge to push him away from me and run out the room so that I can tell my father and Nonna that he's here, and to get help, but I know that I can't. The Crow is too powerful, my family wouldn't be able to do anything for me, he could crush them like bugs if he wanted to. Thankfully the Crow doesn't seem to be that bad of a person. "You are such an amazing person, I love you so much Colomba. I should have told you that a long time ago." He finally releases me from his embrace and his hands go up to his mask so that he can take it off. My eyes grow wide as his fingers touch the mask. This is it! After over two years of battling this guy, I get to finally see his true face and realize who he really is!

"Colomba!" An older man's voice calls out to me, and the Crow's hands immediately fall from his mask. In my excitement it takes me a moment to realize that it is my father's voice.

"Yes Dad!" I can see the feathers on the Crow's wings quivering in his fear that he will be caught in my room by my dad. I can understand why; my dad is usually a really calm person, but if he knew that there was a boy in my room without his permission there would be blood.

"Are you talking to someone in there, I thought I heard someone's voice?" The Crow was scared before, now he looks absolutely terrified. He stares down at me with pleading eyes, silently begging me to not rat him out.

"No Dad, I was just listening to something online, I'm alone." The Crow lets out a faint sigh of relief when I say this and my dad gives me a happy response, feeling better knowing that there is nobody with me.

"Alright Honey, it's time to get some sleep though. We have a busy day ahead of us tomorrow."

"Yes Dad, I will." I quickly say, eager to end that conversation so that the Crow can continue to take off his mask. I am disappointed though. The Crow is staring down at the ground, suddenly looking very defeated.

"I should go." He turns away from me, heading back to my window. Taking a few steps towards him I grab him by the wing, not wanting him to go yet.

"Wait please, don't let my dad stop you from what you were doing. You were determined to show me who you are so we can talk about all of this, please, please don't give up on that now that you are so close." The Crow stops for a moment, possibly thinking about what I said, before he gently takes my hand and removes his wing from my grasp. He still holds my hand when he speaks to me again.

"I can't Colomba, not right now. Please just remember that I love you. No matter what may happen with me or the other people in our school, just remember that I will always love you." Bending over carefully to crawl back out my window, I do not move to stop him, instead I make him stop with a few simple whispered words.

"Crow, please." Those two words come out soft,

almost tearful. I do feel like crying right now, I almost got him to reveal himself to me. After over two years, I almost reached my goal only to have it snatched out of my grasp at the last second. It isn't fair. The Crow seems to misunderstand the reason for the sadness in my voice since he looks like he is about to cry too, knowing that he almost made me cry. Reaching out a gentle hand, he holds my face in his large hand, brushing my cheek with his thumb in a gentle caress. Something in the back of my mind tells me that I need to be afraid, but his soft touch is actually… nice, it feels like I am being comforted by someone I love.

"Do not be sad, my love. I will always be looking out for you, even though you won't know it. I will always be there for you." He moves his face slightly closer to me for a moment, like he wanted to kiss me, but then quickly moved away and rushed out the window. I stick my head out the window as he takes off into the stary sky, heading back to wherever he came from. He leaves me alone wondering what on earth just happened.

Chapter Sixteen
Luis-
The Monster in
The Mirror

I fly above my uncle's shop with our apartment above it for a moment, making sure that there is nobody nearby. When I see that the streets below are empty, without even a single person in sight, I fly down into the alley right behind the shop and transform back into my normal self. I head up the stairs and slip through the window of my room. I do this all silently so that my Uncle Diego doesn't notice. He has never caught me sneaking back into the house after my night flights before, I am now practically an expert at sneaking out.

I flop down on my bed, completely emotionally exhausted after what just happened in Colomba's room. Shadow flies over to the other side of the room and lands on top of my dresser, right in front of the drawing I did of Colomba as the initial sketch for the painting I did for the doctor last year.

Wanting to relax my mind a bit before going to bed, I pull out my sketchbook of all the people I have transformed so that I can draw my monster from earlier today. I easily decide to draw him in his final form, that terrifying mixture of so many creatures. As I sketch, I pay close attention to the skull with the flaming eyes and flame coming out of its mouth. I have to congratulate myself on this one, he was a truly horrifying creation. I frown to myself when I realize the obvious though, even though he was creative he still failed, he gave up the powers I gave him like so many others before him.

Unlike before though, I am not as mad about it this time. I know that when my monster saw that girl in the gym having a panic attack because of him, I know he felt the same way I did, guilty. I guess we do deserve it, we did take things too far. We scared everyone, not just the people who had hurt Rick before. Rick realized that as soon as he saw that girl, he realized that he had become the kind of person he had hated, the people he had wanted to suffer because they were causing an innocent guy like him have panic attacks and make fun of him for them. He hated all these people for that, and yet he did it to an innocent girl who had never even talked to him, let alone make fun of him. I shake my head sadly as I think of that girl's terrified face as I finish the sketch.

When I set the sketchbook down on my bedside table, I look up to see that Shadow is still looking at the picture I had drawn of Colomba. She is looking intently at the image of Colomba in the sketch, a curious look on her face. She almost appears to be examining the image.

"What are you doing Shadow? Is something wrong?" She doesn't even look at me when she gives her response.

"I'm sorry Master, but when I saw Colomba in that dress, she reminded me of someone that I knew. She looks almost exactly like them, I had never noticed the similarity before. They were someone I knew a very long time ago. I just… I miss them." I narrow my eyes in confusion.

"Wait, Shadow, she was dressed like a princess from the Middle Ages, who on earth could she have reminded you of in that dress?" She finally looks back at me as gives me a very simple, yet still very confusing answer.

"She reminds me of someone I knew from the Middle Ages." She turns back around to look at the picture again while I stare at her in disbelief.

"Shadow, how… how old are you?" She looks off into nothingness, a thoughtful expression on her feathery face. After a moment of thought, she answers me.

"Honestly, I do not remember. I lost track a few hundred years ago and never bothered to figure it out again, there doesn't really seem to be a point in knowing how old you are when you can live forever. Maybe one day I will remember, but that is not today. I just know that by the time the Middle Ages were happening when I met the girl Colomba reminded me of, I was still very old by most people's standards." I don't even have anything to say to her after that, I just stare at her in disbelief. In the few years that I have known her, I never would have suspected she was that old. Now that I think about it, I don't really know anything about her. I don't know how old she really is, where she comes from, or even the extent of her powers. I know nothing about the creature I consider to be one of the closest friends I have ever had. That's pretty sad, and I feel ashamed of myself that I never bothered to learn more about my friend. I was always too busy focusing on myself, I have been selfish. Looking back up at her, I look into her black eyes, full of shame.

"Shadow, I'm really sorry that I've never really asked you about yourself. We're supposed to be friends, and I just basically ignored you. I'm really sorry." She hops off the dresser and flies over to me, landing on my shoulder. Shadow uses her beak to push the long bangs out of my face in a motherly gesture.

"It is alright Master, I did not tell you anything because that is something I wish to keep to myself. My past is something you may not understand. Only those who are experienced in magic would truly understand and, sadly, I am the only one left. There are no other magical beings besides myself. They are all gone. All my old friends are gone, they have been gone a very long time." She grows silent for a minute as her head lowers, sadness overwhelming her as she probably thinks of her old friends. After the moment has passed, she looks back up at me, happiness in her dark eyes, but something about this happiness seems a little fake. "I do not wish to focus on my past, but on our present. I do not wish to talk about what has already happened, so you do not need to feel bad about not asking me." Even though I can tell she is trying to smile with her bird face, I can still see the misery behind her eyes.

She really misses these people. I guess if you

have lived as long as she has, then you have watched many people you have cared for die. A dark feeling comes over me when I realize the obvious; Shadow will live long enough to see me die too. I will be an old man one day, and she will live on as a young crow forever. For the first time ever, I feel pity for Shadow. She has probably seen so much but doesn't have anybody to stay with her. Shadow probably has had the loneliest life, and here I am, the guy who's been complaining to her all the time in the few years I've known her about how lonely I am. After hearing what she said though, my problems seem like nothing compared to hers. I know that she said that she doesn't want to talk about it, but now I am extremely curious about her, I want to hear everything. Thing is though, when I look into those sad eyes, I know that I can't. I can't hurt Shadow. She has been a truly great friend to me, and I can't stand the thought of hurting her. I have done a lot in the past that has upset her, and I don't want to do anymore that could make her upset. She deserves better than that, she deserves all the kindness in the world. I smile back at her, but even I can tell that it probably doesn't look like a genuine smile.

"Alright Shadow, I think I'm just going to go to bed, I'm tired after all the stuff that happened tonight." She nods her head, not saying anything, understanding what I mean. Shadow hops off my shoulder and flies back into the Crow Medal leaving me all alone.

As soon as she is gone, I take off my clothes and put on my pajamas. Turning off the lights, I slip underneath the covers on my bed, but I can't fall asleep. My brain has too many thoughts in it to let me.

My mind flashes through everything that happened with Colomba only a few minutes ago. I can't believe I almost showed her my face, what was I thinking? When I think back though about what she said, I can understand why. I felt hope. I felt hope that she could accept me after everything I have done and care for me the same way I care for her. I felt hope then, but I realize that hope was useless now when I think about how my monster turned into me when she saw him. She would never forgive me, she was just trying to see who I really am. She wanted to know who the monster was behind the mask. I look over into my mirror in the darkness. In the image, I see a pathetic kid staring back at me, but if Colomba took off my mask, I know what she would see. She would see betrayal and anger. She would hate the person she sees. She would look at the person behind the mask and hate them forever because she is afraid of them for what they have done. She would see a disgusting human being, if she could even see them as a person anymore. Colomba would look at them and walk away, would never be friends or talk with them again. She would hate me, and I would rather face any torture than live with that. As I sit and feel pity for myself, another person enters my mind, bringing me some confusion.

The image of Alex's face pops into my mind and the instant hate I usually feel when I think of him begins to boil in my stomach. The image is there for only a moment before I see the look on Alex's face when his father had yelled at him after the football game when I had transformed him into the Bull-Y, a look of complete defeat and pain. Then that image changes again so that I can see the look on his face of absolute terror when he saw my creature transformed into his dad. I feel my hands tighten into fists under the blanket in my anger. I let that guy see his worst fear, but his worst fear is something he sees every day of his life. There is not a more terrible torture imaginable that I can think of.

When that realization hits me, the hatred that had been boiling in my stomach slowly dies to be replaced by pure pity. In that moment, I feel myself let go of all the hatred I felt for him all these years, I finally feel myself start to forgive him for everything he has done. Some anger still remains within me, but my forgiveness comes from a sense of pity. I know that he has done terrible things, especially to me, and he did it because he was in pain. That does not excuse his actions, but it certainly makes him more understandable. Sometimes, even the nicest person can lash out at someone when they are angry. If someone is in pain all the time, like Alex is, then it kind of makes sense that he would want to take his anger out on the world. He needs help, and he needs it now.

The anger flares up only slightly when I look over at my Crow Medal. Just because I have forgiven him a little and understand him a bit does not mean that I will let him walk all over me though. I will still fight back in any way I can, and that means using the medal so that he can finally learn that we bullied kids are not ones to be messed with. As I continue to glare at the medal though, my anger fades slowly as I think about my mission and how many times I have failed, yet nothing changes. I feel as if I am on the edge of quitting, why do I keep trying if I always fail? It just makes me look crazy, but I don't want it to look like I gave up though. So many of the outcasts like me look up to the Crow, I can't let them down. While the Medal seems to glow from the dim light of the streetlamp outside my window, I can't help but feel some pain when I look at it. In that medal, I see my pain and my failures. Nothing really good has come out of all of this. Nobody has really changed their minds, everyone still picks on each other even though I have transformed eight people now. My plan has failed, but I can't give up, I can't let the world see me like that. They already see me as the failure as Luis, I can't be a failure as the Crow too.

I turn away from the medal, but I can still feel its presence on my bedside table. The feeling of it seems to mock me as I try to sleep, as if it wants to haunt me in my nightmares. Judging from the bad feeling I have as my eyes begin to close, I can tell that I will be having nightmares tonight.

Chapter Seventeen
Colomba-
A Dark Dream
Haunts Me

After what happened with the Crow in my bedroom, the thought of going to sleep absolutely terrified me, but exhaustion finally caught up to me after the crazy day I've had and my eyes closed so that I could see a beautiful daytime sky in my dreams. I am flying through the sky as a dove again, just like how I have done in dreams a few times before. I have had this dream at least three times now, but I still feel afraid of what is about to happen. I fly through the clouds until I am flying over a building with a courtyard garden in the middle. I fly down to the ground, landing in the middle of the courtyard. In the center is a fountain with the statue of the two boys and a girl, each of them has a bird on their shoulder. Flowers are growing within the garden all along the edge of the building and in other scattered plots in the garden. It is a beautiful place, but I know that the beauty will be ruined by what is about to happen.

I glance to the other side of the garden to see a

weeping willow tree, its branches gently swaying in the soft breeze, brushing the grass beneath it. Within the branches, I can see a small, dark figure hidden behind the branches. My curiosity gets the better of me and I fly through the branches to see a crow standing in front of the tree. I land right in front of the crow and, since I am a tiny dove, the crow looks huge to me. The crow seems happy to see me, he hops over to me and wraps his head around me like he's trying to hug me without arms. The crow looks as if he is in complete bliss holding me, but the happiness does not last.

A shadow falls over us for a moment and we both look up to see that something flying above us had blocked out the sun momentarily. The crow suddenly becomes frightened, I can tell by his ruffled feathers, even though he is trying to hide his fear from me. Looking back up at the flying figure, I can see that it looks like it is getting bigger by the second, but when I take a better look I can see that it is actually getting closer. The crow gets in between the strange shape above us and me, spreading out its wings like they are a shield in front of me. The crow looks back at me and gives out a faint caw, it seems like he is trying to comfort me, to try and tell me to not be afraid of the thing above us because he will protect me. Even though he is terrified, he wants to protect me.

I know by now, since I have had this dream a couple times now, that the crow in front of me in supposed to represent the Crow (obviously), but I am not afraid of him. In fact, I feel a little drawn to him, as if I care about him even though I hate the Crow in real life. I feel comforted by him trying to protect me from whatever that mysterious thing is above us that is making him so scared. When I look up at the mysterious shape that keeps getting closer and closer to us, a strange feeling comes over me that I've had in this dream before too. With that mysterious figure, I have the same feeling of being drawn to it like I do with the crow. I don't know what it is about the figure, but I am not afraid of it even though every thought in my head is telling me that I should be. Something feels wrong about all of this, but I don't know why.

The figure is now pretty close to us and, with my tiny dove size, it looks as if this creature is as big as a house. The crow is practically shaking in front of me in his fear, but he does not budge from his spot in front of me even when the massive creature crashes through the branches of the willow tree with a terrible screech.

Even though I can see the creature more clearly now that the branches are out of the way, it is still shrouded in shadows. What I can make out are that it has massive wings that are bigger than about five of me and these strange, shriveled looking claw like hands that are extended straight toward the crow with sharp dagger like nails. The creature uses those horrific clawed hands to practically swat the crow away from me. When the crow tries to fly back and help me, the creature instead grabs him with its claws and pins him to the ground while I have stayed still out of sheer fear.

The three of us are now completely still, even the crow is as he stays in the grip of this creature, watching me and the creature with fear and curiosity in its gaze, wondering what is going to happen. Even though the creature is right in front of me, I still can't tell what it is since it is covered in shadows like a monster from a nightmare. It stares down at me while I stare up at it, both of us silent, wondering what the other is thinking. This lasts for a minute or two before the creature speaks to me in a deep, yet comforting voice that instantly makes me want to trust it even though I know I shouldn't.

"I will be coming for you soon, my love. I am almost out of here, just wait for me." It stares down at me for a moment before it starts to move its face closer to mine, as if it wants to kiss me. The crow starts to caw and tries to struggle out of the grip of the creature. It looks as if the crow wants to try to rescue me from this creature, but for some reason, I don't want to be rescued. The creature keeps coming in closer and closer to me, almost close enough to kiss me, but I don't want to move, I want to let him kiss me. When we are almost touching, I take a deep breath as I open my eyes to see my room covered in darkness. Glancing over at my bedside table, I can see that it is a little after one in the morning. I groan as I bury my face in my pillow, annoyed that I woke up so early.

As I lay in bed, I think about that dream. It was so strange. I've had this dream several times before, but each time I have it something new is added at the end. This time though, I am more confused than I have ever been after having this dream. What did the creature mean when he said that? Who is he supposed to represent? I know that I am the dove and the Crow is the crow in the dream, but who is the shadowy figure supposed to be? He said that he loves me, so I try to think about all of the people who I know who love me in that way. The Crow seems to have a crush on me, so that's one, but I believe that he is represented by the actual crow in the dream, so it can't be him. So who else loves me? On Valentine's Day I got a lot of cards and gifts where guys were asking me to be their girlfriend because they said that they loved me, but something in my gut tells me that they aren't so important in my life to be in a dream like this one. Only one other person comes to mind when I think about guys who like me, Alex. When I think about the Crow and Alex, I can see how they could match the crow and shadowy figure in my dream. Just like in the dream, the Crow is smaller than Alex physically and would be powerless against Alex if he didn't have his powers. The Crow has mentioned being bullied before, and he transformed Alex into a monster once because he wanted to show me how much of a monster Alex is. I'm guessing that Alex is probably the Crow's biggest bully when he is his usual self. Maybe Alex is supposed to be that creature… but then what did he mean about how he is "almost out of here"? Is he talking about being trapped somewhere? If so, then it can't be Alex. Do I even know who this dark shadow is supposed to be, am I going to meet this person some day and they are currently stuck somewhere trying to get to me?

I shake my head when I realize the obvious, this was just a dream. This isn't something I should be worried about. My dreams aren't some kind of prediction, this is all it is, a strange dream that I keep having. This happens to people sometimes, they have dreams that they keep having repeatedly. I'm doing the same thing. I'm just letting myself get paranoid.

Getting myself settled back into a comfortable position, I try to fall back asleep. Minutes tick by, but sleep does not come due to the thoughts that circle around in my head. Is my dream really nothing? Who is that dark shape? Do I know this person or will I meet them soon? Where are they escaping from? Why do they love me? And if the crow in the dream fears them so much, shouldn't I fear them too? So many questions are asked in my mind, but I have nobody around to answer them tonight. I am all alone in the darkness.

Don't miss the previous books in The Adventures of Silver Dove series.

Eliza Scalia is a therapist who has a master's degree in Clinical Mental Health from Troy University. She enjoys reading, writing, and needlework, as well as hanging out with her pet cat, Dusty. Eliza has been writing since she was in middle school and has self- published the Death's Assistant series for young adults.